"You certainly believe in covering your tracks," Jared said, bitterly.

"Do you blame me?"

Isobel's response was automatic, and she determinedly crushed the emotion she felt when she saw the spasm of pain that crossed his face.

"I guess not," he said at last. "If this is what you really want."

"It is."

"Are you sure?" He stared at her disbelievingly. "God, Belle, if you really don't want to see me again, then I'm going to have to live with it. But was there any need to put the length of the country between us?"

"I think so."

"Why?" he demanded. "Do you really hate me so much?"

She didn't hate him at all; that was the trouble. And Isobel's heart ached at the obvious confusion in his expression.

ANNE MATHER has been writing since she was seven, but it was only when her first child was born that she fulfilled her dream of becoming a published author. Her first book, *Caroline*, met with immediate success and, since then, Anne has written more than a hundred and thirty novels, reaching a readership that spans the world.

Born and raised in the north of England, Anne still makes her home there with her husband, two children and, now, grandchildren. Asked if she finds writing a lonely occupation, she replies that her characters always keep her company. In fact, she is so busy sorting out their lives that she often doesn't have time for her own! An avid reader herself, she devours everything from sagas and romances to suspense.

A *New York Times* bestselling author, Anne Mather has also seen one of her novels, *Leopard in the Snow*, turned into a film.

Books by Anne Mather

HARLEQUIN PRESENTS®

2032—HER GUILTY SECRET
2055—THE BABY GAMBIT
2109—THE MILLIONAIRE'S VIRGIN
2133—INNOCENT SINS
2170—ALL NIGHT LONG

MIRA® BOOKS

DANGEROUS TEMPTATION

Anne Mather

SAVAGE INNOCENCE

HARLEQUIN®

TORONTO • NEW YORK • LONDON
AMSTERDAM • PARIS • SYDNEY • HAMBURG
STOCKHOLM • ATHENS • TOKYO • MILAN • MADRID
PRAGUE • WARSAW • BUDAPEST • AUCKLAND

ISBN 0-373-12207-1

SAVAGE INNOCENCE

First North American Publication 2001.

Copyright © 2001 by Anne Mather.

Visit us at www.eHarlequin.com

Printed in U.S.A.

CHAPTER ONE

IT WAS incredibly hot and airless in the attic. Despite its being a fairly cool July day outside, whatever sun there'd been in recent weeks seemed to have been trapped here in the roof void, and Isobel panted a little as she clambered over trunks and cardboard boxes that hadn't seen the light of day for years.

It was her own fault, of course. She could have refused to do it—though she had to admit she hadn't expected that clearing the house would prove such an arduous task. Sitting back on her heels, surveying the accumulation of what was little more than junk that had collected here over the years, she tried not to feel anxious. But she wondered if she hadn't bitten off more than she could chew.

But there was no one else willing to do it. Marion wouldn't dream of soiling her hands by climbing up here. Besides, as she was always telling Isobel, there simply weren't enough hours in the day to do all she had to do anyway. And Malcolm wouldn't thank her if she gave what little time she had to sorting her late mother's rubbish. Her husband saw little enough of her as it was.

Isobel, who taught at the local comprehensive, was assumed to be able to take a day off to deal with the aftermath of a family bereavement without any problem at all. If her classes had to be covered by someone else, or she got behind in her marking schedule, she'd have to deal with it. Marion had people depending on her, staff, whom she couldn't possibly neglect to dispose of her mother's things.

Isobel supposed it was true. As well as having a husband and an eight-year-old daughter, Emily, Marion also ran her own employment agency. She was always busy interviewing people or attending 'important' meetings. Isobel sometimes wondered why she'd bothered to get married at all.

Isobel wasn't married, which she knew delighted Marion immensely. She knew little of her sister's private life, of course, but the fact that Isobel didn't have a steady boyfriend pleased her no end. Isobel's best friend, Michelle Chambers, said it was because Marion was jealous of her. But why Marion should be jealous of her adopted sister didn't seem to make much sense, in Isobel's view.

Isobel thought Marion was basically unhappy. Despite her assertions to the contrary, she never seemed to enjoy her success. Isobel knew their mother had seen more of Emily than Marion had been able to, and the little girl was going to miss her grandmother terribly.

Mrs Dorland had died six weeks ago. She'd been suffering from a terminal illness for the past three years, so no one was actually shocked by her death. But, for all that, Isobel was amazed at the gulf her mother's loss had left in her life. There was so much she hadn't told her; so much she wanted to tell her now.

Although she'd initially put off Marion's suggestion that the house should be cleared, she'd known that sooner or later she would have to do it. Their father had died some years ago, and although Isobel wasn't married she no longer lived at home, which meant the house in Jesmond Dene was now empty. But she'd known that disposing of her mother's belongings would be painful, and she'd waited until the emotional dust had settled before tackling the job.

Now, however, she didn't have a choice. She was going away herself soon, and Marion was agitating about selling the house while the market was still buoyant. Isobel knew Marion's share of the proceeds was earmarked for the business, and she wished she could insist that her sister had it all.

But the solicitor had been quite adamant on that point. Mrs Dorland's will stated clearly that *both* her daughters should inherit in equal shares. As far as her mother was concerned, she'd never made any distinction between them, and Isobel had sometimes wondered whether that was why Marion had always worked so hard to gain her parents' approval.

It had been easy enough arranging for the furniture to be dealt with. There were firms who specialised in house clearances and, apart from the one or two personal items Isobel had selected, everything else had been despatched to the saleroom.

It was not until Isobel had opened the trap door into the attic that she'd realised the enormity of her task. Unless they were willing to allow strangers to root around in family papers and suchlike, she would have to dispose of these old trunks and boxes herself. Despite the fact that all she'd discovered so far were old clothes and books and photograph albums, she couldn't find it in her heart to just burn them, unseen. There might be something of value. She owed it to her mother's memory to take the trouble to look.

All the same, she hadn't expected it to be so hot up here. And the nausea that had troubled her earlier that morning was beginning to make her sweat all over again. If she didn't get something to eat soon, she was going to start retching, and that was one consequence of her efforts she didn't want to face.

She was crawling back to where the loft ladder pointed down to the first-floor landing when she saw the small dust-covered suitcase. It had been pushed away beneath one of the beams, and it was doubtful if she'd have seen it if she hadn't been on all fours. As it was, she pulled it out, saying a not very ladylike word when the handle came away on one side and a screw scraped her finger. Then, tucking it beneath her arm, she climbed down to the landing below.

First things first, she thought, looping her curly hair behind her ears and descending the stairs to the ground floor. There was no food in the house, but she had brought a flask of coffee and some biscuits with her. Thank goodness, she thought weakly, stuffing a handful of arrowroot fingers into her mouth.

The nausea subsided, as she'd known it would, and, after pouring herself a cup of coffee from the flask, she carried the suitcase into the kitchen. Then, unlocking the back door, she stepped out into the watery sunshine and seated herself on the bench that circled the old apple tree.

This was where her mother used to sit in summer, she remembered sadly. And when she and Marion were schoolgirls, their father had hung a swing from one of its gnarled branches, but that had gone now. Even the blossom, that had flowered so incongruously, she'd felt, just after her mother died, had faded, the grass at her feet strewn with its decaying petals.

Sighing, she thrust her melancholy thoughts aside and turned to the suitcase. It was little more than the size of a briefcase, really, and Isobel couldn't remember ever having seen it before. Perhaps it hadn't belonged to her parents, she thought. Her grandparents had lived in the house before her father and mother were married, so it could have belonged to them. Whatever, it was unlikely to contain anything of importance. All her mother's private papers had been kept by her solicitor.

She thought at first that the case was locked. Her first attempts to flick the twin catches met with no success. But a foray into the toolshed, which still contained some rusty tools and a broken lawnmower, unearthed an old screwdriver, and when she used this to pry at the catches, they gave in.

As she'd expected, the box was just another repository
for papers. Letters this time, postmarked from an address
in Cornwall, all of them at least twenty-five years old.
Isobel frowned. She was not aware that her parents had
known anyone who lived in Cornwall. If they had, neither
of them had ever mentioned it to her. And she doubted
that if Marion had known about it she'd have kept something like that to herself.

Unless...

She shook her head. Were these letters anything to do
with her adoption? She knew virtually nothing about her
real parents. She'd been told that her birth mother had
been killed in a car accident just after she was born, and
that as she'd been an unmarried mother, living alone, her
baby had been taken into care. Isobel had always assumed
that she'd lived in Newcastle, too, which was how the
Dorlands had come to adopt her. Mrs Dorland had always
wanted a large family, but after Marion was born she'd
discovered she couldn't have any more children.

Isobel wondered now why she hadn't asked more questions about her adoption. She supposed the truth was that
her mother had always got very touchy whenever the subject was broached. Isobel had been taught from an early
age that she was lucky to be part of a proper family, and
somehow asking about her birth mother's background was
ungrateful and disloyal.

Which probably had nothing to do with these letters,
she decided, pulling off the elastic band, which had held
them together, and studying the envelope with thoughtful
eyes. It was addressed to her mother, she saw, and her
nerves tightened, needlessly she was sure. She was regarding the letters far too seriously, she thought. They
were probably from a friend her mother had known when
she was young.

She felt a twinge of conscience as she pulled one of the
letters out of its envelope. Perhaps she ought to wait and

ask Marion what she should do with them. But then curiosity, and the knowledge that Marion had eschewed all interest in their mother's effects, encouraged her to investigate further. After all, it was only her imagination that was giving them a significance they probably didn't deserve.

She read the address at the top of the letter first: Tregarth Hall, Polgarron. Impressive, she though wryly, and, even though the letter was old, the quality of the paper was still evident. Then she noticed it started 'Dear *Iris*,' which was her mother's name, and not *Mrs Dorland*. Her unease slackened, and she glanced at the bottom of the page. The signature was Robert *Dorland*. She grimaced. They were obviously from some relation of her father's.

Wondering why that conclusion didn't douse her interest, she turned back to the beginning. *Dear Iris,* she read again, and then went on. *All the arrangements are now in place. Matty will bring the child to you on August 8th.*

The child? Matty?

Isobel's throat went dry, but she forced herself to read on.

I know you consider my actions reprehensible, but there is no way I can keep her even if I wished to, which I do not.

Isobel caught her breath, but she had to go on.

I trust George (her father, Isobel acknowledged tensely) *will learn to live with it. He was always a sanctimonious devil, even in his youth, and, had it not been for your intervention, I am sure the child would have found no favour with him. Still, who am I to judge him? As George would say, I have made my bed, now I should lie on it. He never could forgive anyone's weaknesses.*

*Which is why, I suppose, my father left Tregarth to me,
and not him. I doubt if we'll be in touch again, dear
Iris. My thanks and my best wishes for the future.*

The air escaped from Isobel's lungs in a pained rush,
and the nausea she had defeated only minutes before at-
tacked her again. This time there was no escape. She
barely made it to the downstairs cloakroom before she was
violently sick, and it was several minutes after that before
she was able to drag herself to her feet again.

She felt chilled now. Whereas earlier she had been
sweating in the heat of the attic, now goosebumps feath-
ered her skin. She found the jacket she'd left hanging on
the banister, and pushed her arms into the sleeves, clutch-
ing its warmth about her. But the chill she felt was as
much psychological as physical, and it was some time before she could bring herself to return to the bench.

When she did, she found the dozen or so letters scattered in all directions. They'd tumbled from her lap as
she'd rushed into the house, and, although she was
tempted to toss the lot of them into the dustbin, she forced
herself to pick them up again. Looking at the date of the
postmarks on the envelopes, she discovered that the letter
she'd been reading had been the last one to arrive. They
must have been saved, one on top of the other, in reverse
order, which was how she'd come to read the last letter
first.

And that letter was dated August 1975, which was only
a few weeks after she'd been born. According to her birth
certificate, her birthday was the twelfth of July 1975, and
it was highly improbable that her mother should have been
involved with two babies at that time.

Which meant…? That this man, whoever he was, was
her real father? That he'd got some poor girl pregnant and
then reneged on his responsibilities towards her? Although
George Dorland had always maintained that he had no

relatives, it seemed obvious now that Robert Dorland must be his brother. His younger brother, by the sound of it. And instead of spending his early years in East Anglia, as he'd told his daughters, he'd actually been born in Cornwall instead.

Isobel swallowed, turning the other letters over in her hands. The last thing she wanted to do now was read them, yet she had to know how—*why?*—her own parents hadn't brought her up.

From the tone of the letter she'd read, she thought she could guess at least part of the story. If anything the Dorlands had told her was true, then her mother must have died, as they'd said. But if she'd lived in Newcastle, claiming to be a single mother, how had Robert Dorland become involved with the baby? And who on earth was Matty? Isobel knew from what she'd been told that her real mother's name had been Frances Parry.

She turned, somewhat apprehensively, to the earliest dated letter and drew the two sheets of paper out of the envelope. The address was the same: Tregarth Hall, Polgarron. And it both confirmed Robert Dorland's identity and proved that Mrs Dorland had known him personally.

Dear Iris,
I am writing to you and not to that hidebound brother of mine because I'm hoping that what I have to tell you may strike a chord of sympathy in your heart. Ten months ago, I did something totally selfish and totally stupid. I betrayed Justine by having a brief fling with a young woman I met while I was in London, visiting my solicitor. Believe me when I say that I've regretted it ever since, and I had no intention of having anything more to do with the woman involved. Unfortunately, circumstances have contrived against me, and I now find that a child resulted from that reckless union. How do

I know this? you ask. Because the child's mother has now died, leaving the infant in my care. Not literally, of course. At least, not yet. At present, she is in the care of Southwark Social Services, but I have been contacted, as the child's father, and I fear it's only a matter of time before Justine finds out. You know how distressed she's always been at not being able to have any children herself, and there's no way I can confess the truth to her. I've thought of denying any knowledge of the woman, but who knows what other incriminatory evidence she may have left? No. It's obvious that I've got to find an alternative home for the child, and, knowing how much you and George would have liked a larger family, I'm hoping you might agree to adopt your niece. Yes. In spite of everything, I know she is my daughter. I've seen her, and although her colouring is much darker than mine, the resemblance is there. Naturally, Justine must know none of this. Some other explanation must be found for your decision, but I'm sure we can work something out. What do you think? Will you do this for me? For Justine? For an innocent child? I beg you not to let me down.
Robert.

Isobel was shaking violently when she finished reading the letter. To think, all these years, when she'd believed she had no blood relations, she'd had an aunt, an uncle, a cousin—and a *father*! She couldn't believe it. She didn't want to believe it. Somehow it made a mockery of her life so far.

Why had no one ever told her? Why leave these letters for her to read when for more than twenty-five years she'd been kept in the dark? Surely her feelings had had as much relevance as Justine's? As soon as she was old enough to understand the significance of what had happened, she should have been told the truth.

Stuffing the letter back into its envelope, she reached for the second, and the third, flicking through them with trembling fingers. There were fifteen letters in all, and, however reluctant she was to continue, she knew she had to read them all. Somehow she had to come to terms with what she'd learned, and the only way to do that was to try and understand why it had happened.

But the tenor of the letters changed after that first one. It soon became evident that this was because Robert Dorland's plea had not met with universal approval. George Dorland had apparently refused at first to have anything to do with his brother's problems, and, judging by the response his reaction had earned, there'd been no love lost between the two men.

Slowly, however, perhaps because of Iris's intervention—Isobel would never know now—a compromise had been reached. However opposed to the idea her husband had been, Iris's wishes had prevailed, and he had eventually agreed to adopt the child.

Herself, thought Isobel disbelievingly. She was the child they'd fought over, and, ultimately, she was the one who'd benefited. But at what cost? George Dorland had driven a hard bargain, and his agreement had entailed stringent conditions.

The first was that he'd never wanted to see his brother again. There would be no familial visits; no opportunity for Robert Dorland to secretly drool over his handiwork; to feel a sense of pride in the child he'd been prepared to give away.

The second was that Isobel herself was never to know the truth, which explained her ignorance. Whatever bitterness there'd been between the brothers had been reinforced by her adoption, and was obviously why George Dorland had always denied any connection with his past.

And why she'd never been told she'd been born in London, instead of the north of England.

Spots of rain were dotting the knees of Isobel's leggings by the time she'd snapped the elastic band back around the bundle of letters. Returning them to the case, she closed the lid, and got to her feet. It was odd, she thought, she felt entirely different now from the woman she'd been before she opened the case. Pandora's Box, she thought painfully, as she walked back into the house. She should have burned the letters without reading them as her conscience had prompted her to do.

And yet…

She sighed. Why had her mother kept the letters? She suspected her father hadn't been aware of it, which might account for the fact that the case had been hidden away beneath the beam. It seemed that as far as George Dorland was concerned, his brother had ceased to exist on the day the baby—herself—had been handed over. But Iris had been made of gentler stuff. Was that why she'd hung onto the letters all these years?

Isobel frowned. She wondered if Marion had known anything about it. Did she remember her aunt and uncle, for example? Surely she'd have mentioned them if she had. And when their father died—and their mother—had anyone informed Robert Dorland? Always supposing he was still alive, of course. As the younger brother, it was reasonable that he might be.

The breath caught in Isobel's throat at that thought. My God, she thought. Her father—her real *father*—could still be living in another part of the country. The implications of that conclusion were both thrilling and terrifying. Had Robert Dorland thought about her at all since he'd abandoned her? Goodness, he might not even know that his brother and his wife were dead.

But what if he did…?

She ran a protective hand across the slight mound of

her stomach. Ever since she'd learned of her condition she'd been thinking that history always repeated itself. Like mother, like daughter, she'd thought, but without knowing all the facts. Now, the comparisons between them were even more pertinent. Except... She took a deep breath. She had no intention of putting Jared's name on the birth certificate...

CHAPTER TWO

THE sound of the front door opening brought her round with a start.

She hadn't been aware of leaving the door unlocked, but now she remembered that she hadn't intended to be so long. And if she hadn't opened the trap door into the loft, and realised the amount of work there was still to be done, she wouldn't have been. With the living areas of the house empty of her mother's belongings, she'd thought it was only a matter of tidying up.

How wrong she'd been.

'Belle?'

The attractive male voice was achingly familiar, and, in spite of all the warnings she'd given herself these past weeks, Isobel's heart leapt automatically at the sound. She knew it so well; knew every tone, every nuance, every sensual inflection. Which was why she had to get away, she thought, even though the knowledge pained her. There was no way she could avoid him if she continued to live at the apartment. Or in the area, she acknowledged wryly, even if a future without him in it looked abysmally black at this moment.

'I'm here,' she said, shedding her jacket onto the counter and emerging from the kitchen as Jared Kendall came strolling along the narrow hall. She forced herself to offer him a cool smile, even though she desperately wanted to run away from the temptation he represented. But she had to convince him that their relationship was over, and only by a show of total uninterest could she hope to arouse a similar response.

But God, it was hard, so hard, to disguise the fact that

17

her feelings hadn't changed. Just looking at him, knowing what they had once shared, turned every bone in her body to water. She didn't want to care about him; she *shouldn't* care about him; but she did. And it was that as much as anything that made her resent his coming here.

After the row they'd had two nights ago—the row she'd engineered—she'd been sure it would be several days before he'd attempt to see her again. If he ever did, she'd acknowledged honestly. There was just so much a man— any man—would take.

Yet now here he was, walking towards her with that loose-limbed gait that had always reminded her of the predator he represented. Tall, dark; if it wasn't for the metal-framed spectacles riding on his nose, he'd be every woman's fantasy, and even they only added to his appeal.

Though, to give him credit, he would have hated to think that that was so. Broad shoulders, lean hips, the muscles moving powerfully beneath his tanned skin, he had a toughness that didn't just come from working a good part of his life outdoors. Not handsome, she conceded. His features were too strongly sculpted to fit that image, and one of the first things that had drawn Isobel to him was his total lack of vanity.

But now was not the time to be categorising all his good points, she thought impatiently. Somehow, however painful it might be, she had to make him see that what they'd had was over, finished; before he destroyed them both…

'What are you doing here?' she demanded, wrapping her arms about her midriff in an unknowingly defensive gesture, and Jared arched a sardonic brow.

'Guess,' he said drily, coming to a halt and regarding her with faint resignation. 'If you start with the premise that I wanted to see you, you might come close.'

'Don't make fun of me.'

'Okay.' Jared pushed his hands into the pockets of his leather jacket. 'How about if I say I'm sorry?'

'You're sorry?' Isobel was caught off guard. 'What are you sorry for?'

Jared blew out a breath. 'How the hell do I know?' he exclaimed, revealing he wasn't quite as controlled as he'd like to appear. 'Anything, everything; whatever I've done to make you be like this.'

'Like this?' Isobel latched onto the words. 'Like what? What am I like?'

'Oh, for God's sake!' Jared turned sideways and rested his shoulders back against the wall. 'You know what I mean. Don't insult me by pretending you don't know what I'm talking about.'

'I don't.'

'Oh, right.' He turned his head and gave her a disparaging look. 'So why are we having this argument? Answer me that.'

Isobel was quivering inside, but she had to go on. 'I can't help it if you don't like the things I say,' she declared coolly. 'Just because you can't accept that I might be getting bored with our relationship—'

'That's not true!' He straightened away from the wall, his voice swollen now with anger. 'Our relationship may be many things, not all of them good, I'll grant you, but it's never been boring!'

'So you say.'

'So I know,' he corrected her harshly. He glared angrily at her, his dark eyes smouldering hotly behind the curved lenses of his glasses. 'What is this, Belle? What's happening? Who's been getting at you, for God's sake? Is it your sister? Has she said something to upset you?'

'Why should you think I'd need any encouragement?' Isobel managed to inject exactly the right amount of contempt into her voice. 'Just because you can't accept it, doesn't mean it isn't so.'

Jared wrenched off his glasses and rubbed the bridge of his nose with his forefinger and thumb. Then, taking a deep breath, he composed himself. 'So—what are you saying? That you don't think we should see one another again?'

Isobel felt as if her insides were being rent apart. 'Um—well, yes,' she said tightly. 'I think it would be best for—for both of us. Our relationship isn't going anywhere. And—and I'm not prepared to spend the rest of my life waiting for something that may never happen.'

Jared's face was dark with anguish when she'd finished. Without his glasses, which were still dangling from his hand, he had a vulnerability that wasn't evident when the lenses he wore to correct his short-sightedness were in place. It tore her heart just to look at him, and she wondered what malign fate had decreed that she and Jared should meet.

Which was why she had to go...

'You knew,' he began, his voice thickening with emotion as he spoke, 'you knew I was married when we first began seeing one another. I—never made any secret of the fact.'

'I know—'

'So why are you so impatient now?'

Why, indeed?

Isobel had to steel herself against the almost overwhelming urge she had to go to him then, to comfort him, to tell him that, far from wanting to split them up, she needed him more now than ever. She loved him; she'd known that from the minute she'd backed into his car.

She remembered that day on the supermarket car park now, how he'd uncoiled himself from behind the wheel of the huge Mercedes and come around to see what damage her small Ford had done. She'd expected many things, but not amusement, and his lazy smile had robbed the moment of any sting. She'd been hooked by that smile and by the easy assurance of his manner. The fact that he was also the sexiest man she'd ever seen was just the icing on the cake.

'Perhaps I've changed my mind,' she blurted now. Anything to distract herself from her thoughts. 'It was fun at first—'

'Fun!'

'But I'm not getting any younger. I've decided I—I want a normal life; a normal relationship. I want to get married. Have you thought of that?'

'I think of it all the time,' he retorted bitterly. 'But I'm not free, am I? I thought you understood.'

'I do.'

'It doesn't sound like it.'

'Well, it wasn't meant to sound like that,' she mumbled unhappily. Her heart ached, and she gripped herself tighter. 'I'm sorry.'

'Yeah, I bet you are.'

He shoved his glasses back onto his nose and thrust savage hands through his hair. His hair needed cutting again, Isobel noticed with unwilling tenderness, and there were streaks of grey among its silky dark strands. Were there more now than when she'd first met him? She hoped not, but there was no denying that their affair had taken its toll on both of them.

'So...' He took a deep breath. 'Who is he? Do I know him? Please don't tell me you've been seeing him behind my back.'

Isobel's jaw dropped. 'Who?'

Jared closed his eyes for a moment. 'Belle...' he said, and she could hear the edge of violence in his voice. 'Don't do this to me. You know perfectly well who I mean. This man—this paragon—the one who can give you everything I can't.'

'There is no one else.'

The words were out before Isobel could give any thought to what she was saying. Her denial had been instinctive, and she saw Jared's eyes open again and focus on her with piercing intensity.

'Do you mean that?' He gripped the back of his neck with a bruising hand. 'Or is this what they mean by letting me down lightly?'

Isobel shook her head. Despite the fact that it would be so much easier to pretend that there was someone else, she couldn't do that to him. 'It's the truth,' she said huskily, and then, unable to go on looking at him without revealing what she was trying so hard to hide, she turned back into the kitchen behind her.

Had she known he would follow her? She hardly knew any more. After the morning she had had, she was in no fit state to make any reasoned assessment about anything. Besides, if she was honest she would admit that she had never needed his strength and his commitment more than she did right now. Only he hadn't offered her any commitment, she reminded herself painfully, and she was a fool if she thought he ever would.

She sensed he was behind her even before he touched her. Where he was concerned she had always had a sixth sense, a sensory perception, that she'd used to tell herself proved that their relationship was meant to be. It was as if some energy arced between them, an electrical spark, that was as much spiritual as it was physical, so that when his hands cupped her neck she couldn't prevent the little moan of despair that escaped her. And when his tongue found the pulse that was racing behind her ear, she could only tip her head to one side to facilitate her own destruction.

'God, Belle,' he groaned, his breath cool against her hot skin, and the passion in his voice stroked her flesh with sensual fingers. 'Don't do this to me.'

At that moment it was beyond her capacity to do anything more than stand there, feeling the heat of him at her back, and trying like mad not to lean into him. But it was too much. His teeth had fastened on the skin of her neck now, skin that was the colour of thick cream, and which he had always insisted was just as rich and smooth, tugging the soft flesh into his mouth. There'd be a mark there now, she knew it, but she would willingly have stripped all the skin from her bones if it would have pleased him. She loved him. Ah, God, she was crazy about him. He had no idea what it was costing her to leave him.

His hands slid down her arms to her hands, linking their fingers together. Then, with just the slightest pressure, he urged her slim body to mould itself to his, his legs parting so that she was instantly aware of his arousal against her bottom. She was a tall girl herself, and Jared had always said they fitted one another perfectly.

She trembled then, and, sensing her weakening state, Jared uttered a muffled oath as he turned her towards him. Cradling her face between his palms, he stroked the faint shadows that had only recently appeared beneath her eyes with his thumbs, before tilting her head to his.

'I need you,' he said unsteadily, and she believed him. Their relationship would never have survived as long as it had without the friendship that had flowered between them. This past year had been the happiest time of her life, and if that damned her soul for all eternity, given the chance she'd do it all again.

He bent to kiss her, their mingled breaths causing the lenses of his glasses to film over, and Isobel lifted her hand to remove them. Her lips parted under the increasing pressure of his mouth, and when his tongue plunged deeply into that moist void, she clutched his glasses as if they were the only stable thing in a wildly unstable world.

Jared's hands moved down her back to her hips, bringing her more fully against him, the thrust of his erection nudging the junction of her thighs. His fingers shaped the rounded swell of her buttocks, finding the cleft that divided them easily through her thin leggings, and causing Isobel to arch helplessly against his insistent strength.

'I want you,' he told her thickly, his words barely audible as his mouth returned to hers with more urgency, and although she knew she was playing with fire, she wound her arms around his neck.

'Not here,' she got out jerkily, as her only concession to her departing sanity, but Jared seemed intent on proving to her that she wanted him just as much as he wanted her.

'Why not?' he demanded, his fingers slipping beneath the hem of her man-size tee shirt to find the softness of her bare flesh. He stroked her midriff with caressing hands, before seeking the unfettered freedom of her small breasts. 'It's what I want; it's what we both want.'

'No—'

'Yes.' He teased the sensitive nipples that swelled against his palms, and then peeled her tee shirt upward, exposing the rosy areolae to his possessive gaze. 'God, Belle, you can't stop me now!'

One hand curved along her thigh, bringing her leg up around his hips and lifting her off her feet. Realising what he intended to do, Isobel wrapped her other leg about his waist. It brought the sensitive place between her legs even closer to the taut seam of his trousers, and she was hardly aware that he'd carried her into the kitchen until he set her on the lip of the counter. Then, while she put his glasses aside and rested back on her hands, he peeled the close-fitting leggings down to her ankles.

When he spread her thighs and moved between them, she was more than ready for him, and her breathing quickened when the thickness of his erection probed her moist core.

But, just as she was giving herself over to the treacherous delight of feeling him a part of her again, he swore softly and drew back. 'Damn, I don't have anything with me,' he muttered. He groaned. 'I don't normally go to work with a pocket full of—well, you know what I mean.'

'It doesn't matter.'

Isobel's words were frantic, revealing how hopelessly eager she was, and Jared stared at her with dark, tormented eyes. 'Do you mean that?' he asked unsteadily. 'Is it the right time of the month or something?'

'Or something,' she agreed weakly, remembering another occasion when she had assured him that it was safe to take the risk. Of course it hadn't been so, which was why…

But she didn't want to think about that now, and, reaching down, she guided him towards her aching flesh. 'Just do it,' she said, and as she'd expected—as she'd *known*—Jared was not immune to such flagrant provocation, and he sighed with pleasure as he surged into her wet sheath.

'God, Belle,' he moaned, as her muscles tightened around him, and because she was no longer in control of herself, or her emotions, Isobel cupped his face in her hands and brought his open mouth to hers.

She thought she might have been content then just to know he was there, buried deep inside her, but as soon as he began to move she knew that being there wasn't enough. She wanted more, she wanted him, she wanted all of him, and his breathing grew hoarse and laboured as the irresistible demands of the flesh drove him to take them both to a glorious climax.

They came together, and Isobel felt the exquisite heat of Jared spilling his seed inside her. There was nothing to touch it. She sighed. The blissful union of male meeting female, skin to skin, flesh to flesh. The ripples of their lovemaking left them both shuddering in the aftermath, and Isobel would have liked nothing better than to spend the rest of the afternoon here or at her apartment, with Jared, repeating their closeness again and again.

But a chilling sense of reality returned when Jared bestowed one last lingering kiss at the corner of her mouth, and then drew away from her. While he fastened his trousers, she shuffled awkwardly off the edge of the counter, and bent to haul her leggings, and the bikini briefs he'd pulled down with them, up her legs.

'Are you okay?' he asked huskily, watching her, and she was warmed by the look in his eyes which told her he had been as reluctant to break their embrace as she was.

But that didn't alter the situation, and, making the excuse of needing to use the bathroom, she slipped into the cloakroom next door.

A glance at her reflection didn't help either. No one looking at her flushed face and swollen lips could be in any doubt as to what had been going on, and she wished she'd brought her make-up with her. Her hair, lustrous chestnut hair, which she usually wore short these days in an effort to quell its urge to curl, was a tousled mass about her creamy features. She looked—wanton, she thought unhappily. Which was not the image she'd wanted to convey.

She stayed in the cloakroom as long as she dared, and when she emerged she found Jared waiting for her in the kitchen. His hips were propped against the counter, where he had just made such passionate love with her, his arms folded across his broad chest, his glasses back in place.

The suitcase containing the letters she had been examining earlier—and which she had almost forgotten in the heat of their mating—was lying on the counter at his back, and he tipped his head towards it in obvious enquiry.

'Whose is this?'

Recognising the tension in his casual query, Isobel wondered if he thought it was hers. A hysterical sob rose in her throat at the unknowing irony of that suspicion, but she managed to fight it back, and, sliding her long fingers into the sides of her hair, she lifted her shoulders in a dismissing gesture.

'It was my mother's.'

Jared's dark brows drew together. 'Your mother's?' he echoed. 'I thought you'd got rid of all your mother's stuff.'

'I thought so, too.' Isobel took a deep breath. 'That was before I looked in the loft.'

'The loft? Here?' Jared glanced towards the ceiling. His eyes darkened. 'You haven't been crawling around in the loft on your own?'

Isobel gave him a retiring look. 'Someone has to do it,' she said drily.

'Not on your own,' retorted Jared, evidently disliking the proposition. He flicked back his cuff and looked at the plain gold watch on his wrist. 'Dammit, I've got to go. I've got a meeting with Howard and Ross Cameron at half-past one.'

'And it wouldn't do to keep your father-in-law waiting, would it?'

Isobel couldn't resist the mocking comment, and she saw the look of real pain that crossed his face. 'No, it wouldn't,' he conceded flatly. 'Particularly as he can probably smell you on me,' he said, straightening away from the bench, and Isobel felt instantly ashamed.

'Um—you could take a quick shower,' she offered, gesturing towards the stairs. 'I think there's an old towel still up there—'

'Did I say I cared?' Jared demanded, coming to slide caressing hands over her shoulders. He angled his head to rest his forehead against hers. 'Dammit, Belle, I don't want to go.'

She didn't want him to go either, but even thinking such a thought was breaking every promise she'd made to herself, and she knew she had to stop wishing for miracles. They didn't happen, and somehow she had to get over it—get over *him*—and move on.

Move on...

God, how cold that sounded. Isobel felt the prick of

unshed tears burning behind her eyes and she knew she
had to make him go before he started suspecting that
something was seriously wrong.

'I'll see you tonight, right?' he murmured, kissing her
again, but Isobel shook her head.

'Not tonight,' she said, through dry lips. 'I—I've got
too much to do. I've got to finish here, and then I've got
some marking—'

'You're not going into that loft again,' said Jared
harshly. He tipped her face up to his. 'Promise me you
won't go up there unless someone else—preferably me—
is with you.'

Isobel expelled an unsteady breath. 'I—all right,' she
agreed, deciding that, whatever else was left up there,
Marion's husband would have to move it. She forced a
smile. 'You'd better go.'

'Okay.' Jared released her without further protest and
started towards the door. 'I'll ring you,' he said, pausing
at the end of the hall, and then, with an irrepressible grin,
he let himself out of the door.

She cried after he'd gone. She told herself her hormones
were responsible, that ever since she'd found out what was
wrong with her she'd been in a state of emotional turmoil,
but she knew she was just fooling herself. She wasn't crying because she was pregnant. She was crying because
he'd never know.

Then, as she went to the sink to bathe her eyes with
cool water, her gaze alighted on the suitcase again. And
suddenly she knew what she was going to do. She'd
planned on leaving Newcastle, but until now she'd had no
clear idea of where she was going to go. The little money
she'd saved and her share from the sale of the house would
support her until she found a regular job, and she considered herself lucky to have an occupation that was not confined to any one area. Oddly enough, she'd thought of
moving south and west, and now she knew her destination.

She was going to Cornwall, to a town not too far distant
from Polgarron, wherever that was. And she was going to
do her best to find out what kind of man her father was—
or had been...

CHAPTER THREE

WHEN someone knocked at the door of her apartment that evening, Isobel's heart leapt into overdrive. She was expecting Michelle, but it was too early for her, and she wondered how she'd explain her friend's arrival to Jared if it was him. When she'd told him she couldn't see him, it had been because she'd planned to spend the evening packing things that would be put into storage until she found somewhere else to live. Michelle had agreed to help her, despite her own misgivings about Isobel's decision.

But when she eventually opened the door, she found her sister waiting on the landing outside. 'I was beginning to think you weren't in,' remarked Marion tersely, brushing past her into the living room. She loosened the jacket of her black business suit and glanced about her impatiently. 'What's going on?'

Isobel closed the door, a frown drawing her dark brows together as she followed Marion into the room. 'What do you mean?' she asked, her pulse palpitating at the thought that Marion might have somehow found out about what she intended to do. A quick glance assured her that she'd disposed of all the evidence. So long as her sister didn't go into the spare bedroom, she appeared to be safe.

'You were going to call at the agency after you'd finished at the house,' Marion reminded her shortly, and Isobel breathed a little more easily. After reading Robert Dorland's letters, and the disturbing emotions aroused by Jared's visit, she'd forgotten all about the promise she'd made to her sister.

'I—forgot,' she said lamely now, and Marion regarded her with scarcely concealed irritation.

'How could you forget?' she exclaimed, subsiding onto a braided sofa. 'You knew I'd promised to give the keys to the estate agent this afternoon.'

'Yes, well...' Isobel sighed. 'There's a problem.'

'A problem?' Marion looked sceptical. 'You haven't found something structurally wrong with the house, have you?'

'No.' Isobel shook her head. 'Why should you think that?'

Marion shrugged, and then, when it became apparent that Isobel expected an answer, she clicked her tongue. 'If you must know, Malcolm saw Howard Goldman's son-in-law going into the house at lunchtime,' she said shortly.

'Oh.' Isobel felt the heat in her cheeks, and she turned away towards the kitchen. 'Can I get you something to drink? Tea? Or something stronger? I think I have some sherry. And beer, of course—'

'Nothing, thanks.' Marion's lips were tight. 'You do know the risk you're taking, don't you, Isobel?' She shook her head. 'If Elizabeth Kendall finds out...'

'She won't.' Isobel pushed her hands into the back pockets of her jeans. She'd had a shower when she got back from the house and deliberately changed her clothes in an effort to forget what had happened. 'In any case, we were talking about something else—'

Marion ignored her. 'I thought you told me you'd finished with Jared Kendall.'

Isobel felt a flare of indignation at her sister's careless intrusion into her private affairs. She and Jared had been seeing one another for over six months before Marion had found out about their relationship, but ever since she had she'd been warning Isobel of the dire consequences, not just to her, but to Marion's agency, if Howard Goldman discovered the truth.

'Let's leave it, shall we?' Isobel suggested flatly, and, as if sensing she was on shaky ground, Marion contented herself with sniffing her disapproval. 'I was talking about what I found in the loft.'

'The loft?' She had Marion's attention now. 'What's the loft got to do with anything?'

'It's full of junk,' said Isobel evenly. 'At least, that's all I thought it was.'

'What do you mean?'

Marion looked genuinely puzzled, and Isobel walked across the room and extracted the bundle of letters from the suitcase she'd left hidden behind an armchair. Handing her sister the letter she'd seen first, she said, 'Read that.'

Marion frowned, handling the envelope as if its evident age and discoloration offended her sensibilities. 'What is it?'

'Read it,' urged Isobel, endeavouring to control her impatience, and Marion pulled a face as she extracted the letter.

'Very well,' she said, flicking a speck of dust from her fingers. 'But I can't imagine why you would think...'

Her voice trailed away as she began to read. Watching her expression, Isobel soon became convinced that what she was seeing was as much of a shock to Marion as it had been to her. Her sister looked up once, when she was about halfway through the letter, and gave Isobel a disbelieving stare, but she waited until she'd reached Robert Dorland's signature before making any comment.

'Do you think this has something to do with you?'

Isobel shrugged. 'Don't you?'

Marion looked down at the letter again. 'How would I know? Who is this Robert Dorland? Some relation of Daddy's, I suppose.'

'His brother,' Isobel told her. She flicked through the other letters she was holding. 'I've read all of these, and that one was the last.'

Marion held out her hand. 'Can I read them?'

'Of course.' Isobel handed them over. 'But not now. I—well, I'm expecting somebody.'

Marion's expression tightened. 'Not Jared Kendall?'

'No, not Jared,' agreed Isobel wearily. 'Though if he was coming here, it would be nothing to do with you.'

'It would if his father-in-law found out I'd known about it, and done nothing to try and put a stop to it.'

Isobel caught her breath. 'Marion, you're not my keeper.'

'No, but Howard and Elizabeth are friends,' declared Marion, fitting the letter back into the envelope. 'We've even had dinner with them occasionally.'

'Very occasionally,' remarked Isobel drily. Howard Goldman and the Rimmers happened to belong to the same golf club, and Marion had been trying for years to cultivate the right kind of social circle. So far their contact with the Goldmans had been restricted to charity dinners and the like, but Marion had ambitions.

'Nevertheless—'

'Nevertheless, nothing,' said Isobel shortly. She squared her shoulders. 'Did you know anything about this?'

'This?' Marion held up the letter. 'No. How could I?'

'You've never heard of Robert Dorland?'

Marion was indignant. 'Isobel, I was only three years old when Mum and Daddy adopted you.'

'Yes.' Isobel acknowledged what she'd already accepted herself. 'So what do you think I should do?'

'Do?' Marion blinked. 'What do you mean? What do *I* think you should do? What can you do? These letters are—what? Twenty-five, thirty years old?'

'I'm only twenty-six, Marion.'

'Oh, yes. Right.' Marion pulled a wry face. 'Well, it hardly matters now.'

Isobel dropped down into the armchair opposite. 'Don't you think so?'

'How could it? This man—this Robert Dorland—is probably dead by now.'

'He might not be.'

'No.' Marion conceded the fact with ill grace. 'But what are you going to do? Turn up on his doorstep and expose the secret he's been keeping all these years: you!'

'He is my father.'

'Is he?'

'Of course he is.' Isobel stared at her. 'Surely you don't think he'd have gone to all that trouble if—'

'Oh, I'm sure he *thought* he was your father,' declared Marion dismissively. 'But your mother was hardly a paragon of all the virtues, was she? I mean—' Her lips twisted, and Isobel could almost see what she was thinking. 'Getting involved with a married man! How do you know she wasn't lying about your paternity in the hope of making a better life for herself?'

'Because Robert Dorland wouldn't even have known he had a daughter if she hadn't been killed,' retorted Isobel tersely. 'For pity's sake, Marion, what are you implying here?'

'Well, you don't know anything about her, do you? She could have been—well, anything.'

Isobel sprang to her feet. 'I think you'd better go now.'

'Oh, Isobel, don't be so melodramatic.' But Marion got to her feet anyway, clearly aware that she had overstepped the mark. 'All right. Maybe I'm not being very—sympathetic about her, but you know I don't mean anything by it. It's just my way.'

'Yes.' Isobel knew Marion's ways very well. She snatched the bundle of letters out of her sister's hands and folded them within her arms. 'Well, I don't think you'll be needing these,' she said, stepping aside so that Marion could walk towards the door. She took a breath. 'Oh, and here are the keys,' she added, lifting them off the table by the door. 'But you'll have to get Malcolm or somebody else to clear out the rest of the junk. There's far too much for me to handle.'

'Isobel…'

Marion tried again to placate her sister, but Isobel had had as much as she could take for one day. 'I'll be in touch,' she said, guiltily, aware that she was planning to leave town without giving her sister her new address. 'Goodnight.'

'Goodnight.'

Marion took the keys and left, but after she'd gone Isobel found herself in tears again. Dammit, she thought, what was wrong with her? The sooner she got out of Newcastle the better.

She'd barely dried her eyes before Michelle arrived. Her friend came into the apartment looking at Isobel with anxious eyes. 'What's wrong?'

Isobel sighed. 'Don't ask.'

'Jared Kendall,' said Michelle disgustedly, taking off her jacket. 'Honestly, Issy, I thought you were going to be sensible about him.'

'I am being sensible.'

'Oh, right.' Michelle flicked her neck with a sardonic finger. 'So what's this? A mosquito bite?'

Isobel covered the mark Jared's teeth had made with defensive fingers. 'Jared hasn't upset me,' she denied. 'It was Marion, if you must know.'

'Oh, yeah?' Michelle flopped down onto the sofa, spreading her ample bulk over both cushions. 'So what's she done now?'

Isobel hesitated. 'I found some old letters in the loft today.'

'Big deal.' Michelle pulled a face. 'Isn't that what you usually find in lofts? Old papers; old letters; *junk*? What's that got to do with the green-eyed monster?'

'The letters were from my father.'

'So?'

Isobel sighed. 'My *real* father!'

Michelle frowned. 'Your real father?' She shook her head. 'I thought you didn't know who your real father was.'

'I didn't. Until today.' Isobel looked doubtful. 'It turns out he was my father's brother.'

'Are you serious?' Michelle's blue eyes were wide. 'Holy Moses! And they never told you?'

'They didn't tell anyone,' said Isobel unhappily. 'My father—my adoptive father, that is—made that a condition when he agreed to take me.'

Michelle still looked confused. 'But I didn't know your father had a brother.'

'Nor did I.'

'And your real mother—?'

'She's still dead.' Isobel looked wistful now. 'It turns out that when she was killed the authorities discovered that she'd named Robert Dorland as—as my father.'

'*Robert* Dorland?'

'That's right.'

'So where is he now?'

'I'm not sure. At the time the letters were written, he was living at somewhere called Tregarth Hall in Polgarron. That's in Cornwall.'

'Cornwall?'

'Mmm.' Isobel nodded. 'It turns out I was born in London, not Newcastle.'

'I don't believe it!' Michelle was amazed.

'Of course, the facts of—of my adoption are the same. My mother was still unmarried at the time I was born. Her—association with my father was very brief.'

She was feeling weepy again now, and when she turned away to go into the kitchen Michelle sprang up from the couch and went after her. 'Hey,' she said, putting her arm about the other woman's shoulders. 'It's nothing to cry about. At least you know who you are now.'

'Do I?'

'Sure you do.' Michelle sighed, searching for the right words. 'Are you telling me Marion knew about this all along?'

'I don't think so.' Isobel drew away from her, pulling a tissue out of the box she kept on the counter and blowing her nose before going on. 'She seemed as shocked as me.'

'Then, what—?'

'Oh, it was something and nothing,' said Isobel tiredly. 'She suggested that Robert Dorland might not be my father after all. That my mother might just have used his name—'

'To what advantage?'

'That's what I said,' said Isobel eagerly. 'I mean, if she hadn't been killed, he would never have known.'

'Precisely.' Michelle snorted. 'For goodness' sake, don't let her upset you. As I've said many times before, she's a jealous cow.'

'But why?' exclaimed Isobel blankly. 'She's the success of the family, not me.'

'Well, obviously she doesn't think so,' retorted her friend shrewdly. 'It must have been a sickener for her when she found out about you and Jared. I mean, doesn't she spend all her time trying to insinuate herself with the divine Elizabeth?'

'Don't say that.' Isobel couldn't allow Michelle to ridicule Jared's wife. 'Life hasn't been easy for Elizabeth, you know that.'

Michelle grimaced. 'I know what she wants everyone to believe,' she remarked drily. 'But, okay. I won't say anything bitchy about Mrs Kendall if you'll stop getting mopey over Marion's maliciousness. Hell, she's probably afraid you're going to go looking for him.'

Isobel frowned. 'Why should that bother her?'

'Come on.' Michelle was impatient now. 'What was that address you just told me? Tregarth Hall? That doesn't sound like a semi in a nice, but unspectacular, part of town.'

Isobel stared at her. 'You're saying you think my father might be a—a wealthy man?'

'It's possible,' said Michelle, shrugging as she opened Isobel's fridge. 'Ah, wine,' she noted approvingly. 'I thought you'd never ask.'

Isobel sniffed again, but her mouth tilted a little at her friend's good-humoured common-sense. 'I don't want any,' she said, helping herself to a can of Coke. 'It's all yours.'

Michelle lifted the bottle out of the fridge and looked for the corkscrew. 'So you're really going through with this, then?'

Isobel looked down at her stomach. 'You mean the baby?'

'I mean the baby,' agreed Michelle, pouring herself a glass of Chardonnay. 'Does Marion know about that?'

'Heaven forbid!' Isobel spoke fervently. 'She'd say, Like mother, like daughter.'

'Mmm.' Michelle headed back into the living room. 'And you're still determined that Jared doesn't need to know either?'

Isobel nodded vigorously. 'It was never meant to happen, Michelle. You know that. It'll be better for all of us when I go away.'

'Well, if you want my honest opinion, I think he's bloody lucky to have known you,' declared her friend staunchly. 'I hate to say anything good about the bastard, but he hasn't had the happiest of marriages with the—with Elizabeth, has he?'

'No.' Isobel's throat was tight.

'And, contrary to what you say, I think he would do something about it, if he knew.'

'What? Get a divorce? I don't think so. Apart from the

fact that Elizabeth's disabled, it's common knowledge that he was driving the car when the accident happened.'

Isobel was getting emotional again, and Michelle apparently decided it was time to back off. 'Who knows?' she said lightly. 'What he doesn't know won't hurt him, I guess.' She sank down onto the sofa again, and took a sip of her wine. 'So...what are you going to do about the letters?'

Isobel perched on the chair opposite. 'What do you think I should do?'

Michelle arched improbably thin eyebrows. 'How should I know?' Her eyes narrowed. 'But I guess, looking at you now, that you've got a plan in mind.'

'I had,' admitted Isobel ruefully. 'Now, I'm not so sure.'

'Why not?'

Isobel bit her lip. 'I had thought of looking for somewhere to live near—near Polgarron.'

'Ah. And?'

'Well, if your suspicions are true, and he—does have money, I don't want him to think I'm looking for him now because I think he—owes me something.'

'He does.'

'Michelle!'

'He does, dammit. You are his daughter.'

'If it's true.'

'Do you doubt it?'

'No.'

'There you are, then.' Michelle was triumphant. 'I suggest we drive down the first weekend of the holidays.'

Isobel caught her breath. 'You'll come with me?'

'And see you settled? What else?'

'Oh, Michelle, thank you.' Isobel went and gave her friend an impulsive hug. 'I thought I'd have to go on my own.'

'How are you going to haul all your stuff in that matchbox of yours?' demanded Michelle, disparaging Isobel's car with affectionate familiarity. 'No, we'll take the estate car. Phil can manage with my car for a few days, and we'll leave your car in our garage until you're settled. Then, you can either come back for it or get a local garage to deliver it for you.'

Isobel shook her head. 'Won't Phil object?' Michelle's husband was a sales rep and used the estate car to carry demonstration equipment.

'As I say, he can make do with the Peugeot. Honestly, he won't mind.'

'But your holiday—'

'We're not going away until the third week in August,' exclaimed Michelle impatiently. 'Stop making obstacles where there aren't any. With a bit of luck, you'll be installed in your new place before we go away. Hey—' she laughed '—after you move, Phil and I will have a permanent holiday home in the West Country, won't we?'

'The West Country.' Isobel echoed the words with a shiver of apprehension. Despite the news about her father, and the gratitude she felt towards Michelle for her help and understanding, she couldn't forget what she was leaving behind. 'It sounds so far away.'

'It is far away,' said Michelle mildly. 'I thought that was the idea.'

Isobel heaved a sigh. 'It is, of course, but—'

'You're going to miss me. I know,' said Michelle drily, but when Isobel turned pained eyes in her direction, she shook her head in knowing resignation. 'You've got to forget him, kid. You said yourself there's no future in it.'

'That doesn't stop me wishing—' Isobel cut herself off before she could finish the damning sentence and swung around towards the spare bedroom. 'Come on. Let's get started with the packing. It's only two weeks to the start of the summer holidays.'

CHAPTER FOUR

JARED dropped his hard hat onto the seat beside him, and rested his head against the soft leather upholstery. It had been a long, hot day and the hair at the back of his neck was damp with sweat. He needed a drink and a shower, not necessarily in that order, and then the prospect of spending the rest of the evening with the only woman he cared anything about.

Isobel...

But that wasn't going to happen. He scowled as he started the engine of the powerful Mercedes, barely acknowledging the salute of the security guard who was on duty at the gate of the building complex. Elizabeth had a dinner party for her father planned that he'd promised to attend. Instead of changing into jeans and a tee shirt and picking Isobel up for a bar-meal at some country pub, he was obliged to put on a dinner jacket and spend several hours talking to people he didn't even like.

He sighed. That wasn't absolutely true. Many of his in-laws' acquaintances were friends of his, too, and if he could have counted on looking at Isobel across the candlelit dinner table he'd have been content.

He was actually working on a plan to take her away for a few days. There was an architects' conference in Paris in August, and the prospect of several days—and nights—with Isobel caused his trousers to become unpleasantly tight. Dammit, they'd never spent a whole night together. He couldn't wait to wake up with her beside him.

The trouble was, while it was comparatively easy to find excuses for going out in the evenings, it was much harder to explain a night's absence. And, lately, Isobel had been finding excuses for not seeing him in the evenings either. On two or three occasions recently she'd turned him down in favour of other commitments, and, while he knew she had some crazy idea of breaking up with him, he also believed she was as helpless as he was to destroy what they shared.

His lips twisted. It was his own fault, after all. No one had forced him to marry Elizabeth. He'd gone into their relationship with his eyes open, and if the knowledge that as Howard Goldman's son-in-law he might be given the opportunity to gain recognition for his work had not been unpleasing to him, it had definitely not been the sole reason he'd made Elizabeth his wife.

He'd joined Goldman Lewis as a very junior draughtsman after getting his degree, and from the beginning he'd been aware of Howard Goldman's daughter watching him every time she came into the office. Elizabeth was easy on the eye, and he wouldn't have been human if he hadn't been flattered by her attention, but he'd never expected anything to come of it.

That it had had been more due to Elizabeth than himself. Young architects with big ideas were ten a penny, and he'd naturally assumed that Elizabeth would marry someone with a far different pedigree than his own. He'd actually hesitated before accepting that first invitation to a party at the Goldmans', unsure what her father would make of one his junior employees fraternising with the boss's daughter.

In fact, Howard Goldman had encouraged the relationship, but it hadn't been until they were married that Jared had found out why. Dazed by the speed with which he'd been promoted from a minor employee of the firm to a member of the family, Jared hadn't looked for reasons. He'd been far too busy congratulating himself on his good fortune to search for motives for his success.

His life with Elizabeth, however, had soon proved how naïve he had been. The woman he'd known far too fleetingly before the wedding bore little resemblance to his new wife, her black moods and violent depressions demonstrating that whatever feelings she had expressed for him before they were married, she could barely tolerate him now.

Within a few months, Jared had realised that Elizabeth's reasons for marrying him had had nothing to do with love or sex. She'd no longer been interested in him except as a means to pacify her father, and Jared had begun to understand that marrying him had been a way to get Howard off her back. The old man had confided in him before the wedding that his dearest wish was that his daughter should give him a grandchild, and, with Elizabeth approaching her thirtieth birthday, he'd been losing hope that she'd ever find a husband. Now that they were going to get married, he'd assumed Elizabeth would be proud to grant his wish.

How wrong he'd been.

Jared's lips compressed. Elizabeth's agenda had been totally different from her father's, from his own. She'd known all about his background before the wedding: the fact that his parents were dead, that he'd been brought up in a series of foster homes until he was sixteen and he'd run away to London, that there'd been little love of any kind in his life. He'd had to steel himself against his emotions; he'd been hurt too many times in the past to trust anything to change. He'd worked at a handful of jobs to earn the money to go to college, determined to get the qualifications necessary to get a decent job. And when he'd passed all his exams he'd returned to the north-east.

To a job with Goldman Lewis.

He sighed now. Elizabeth had apparently believed he'd be so grateful to her for what her father could do for him that whatever she did, however she behaved, he wouldn't object. She'd been sure he'd do nothing to jeopardise his privileged position, but she couldn't have been more wrong. For more than half his life already he'd been forced to do what other people—often strangers—told him, and he'd had no intention of allowing it to happen again.

Yet it had.

He scowled. He'd tried so hard to save the marriage, he remembered bitterly. He'd even convinced himself that he must be to blame for Elizabeth's change of attitude towards him, and when she'd suggested that their relationship might benefit from being given a little space, he'd happily agreed to her spending the weekend at a health farm with one of the women she played golf with.

The call that had shattered all his illusions had come on a Sunday morning. Jared had been sprawled on one of the sofas in the living room, the Sunday papers scattered around him in disarray. He'd actually been anticipating his wife's return with some enthusiasm, hoping against hope that whatever it was that had brought them together might still have the power to promote a reconciliation.

The call had killed any feelings he'd still had for her. It had been from a clinic in London. To begin with, Jared had assumed Elizabeth must have given him the wrong information. She'd said the health farm was in Northamptonshire, and as these places sometimes called themselves clinics, Jared had assumed he'd made a mistake.

He hadn't.

The young woman who'd contacted him—a very junior nurse, he'd learned later—had explained that there'd been a complication. She'd said that the operation Mrs Kendall had had the previous afternoon hadn't gone as satisfactorily as Dr Singh had anticipated.

Jared had been stunned. He hadn't known Elizabeth needed an operation and he'd briefly blamed himself for his ignorance. And when he'd expressed his concern the young nurse had taken pity on him, assuring him that his wife was in no danger, that the termination had been successful.

Jared had heard the rest of what she'd said in numbed disbelief. He hadn't wanted to hear that Elizabeth had developed an infection immediately after the operation, or that she wouldn't be able to return to Newcastle for a few days. His revulsion that she should do such a thing, without even telling him, had been all he could think about, and he'd been hard pressed to be civil to the girl who'd broken the news.

Of course, Elizabeth had never expected him to find out. As he'd discovered afterwards, the clinic was supposed to be totally confidential, and it was only the fact that a new—and very inexperienced—nurse had been on duty when Elizabeth had expressed her concern about the delay, and had taken it upon herself to call the number Elizabeth had given when she'd booked in, which had given the game away. Elizabeth herself had been a little groggy at the time, or she'd never have made such a stupid mistake. She'd have waited until she was well enough to call him herself, and given some other excuse for not returning home.

Jared didn't know how he'd got through the rest of that day or the days that followed. His first impulse had been to pack his bags and be out of there before his wife got back, but he'd wanted to see her first, to tell her what he thought of her, and that had been a mistake. When Elizabeth had got back she'd been still weak and shaken, but not too weak to remind him of the effect his intended actions would have on her father. The infection she'd developed after the abortion meant there could be no second chances, and the thought of Howard finding out that his daughter would never give him a grandchild was not a prospect Jared had wanted to face.

He'd been brought brutally back to earth when Howard had reminded him of the dinner he and Elizabeth were expected to attend in Alnwick the following evening. Howard had been invited, but it had clashed with another engagement he had in the city, and because these days Jared often acted as his deputy, the Kendalls had been invited in his stead.

The arrangements had been made weeks before or Jared wouldn't have hesitated in turning the invitation down. But to do so would have created questions he had not yet been ready to answer, and for Howard's sake he hadn't made any complaint.

Only when Elizabeth had insisted on driving home after the dinner had Jared objected. Knowing he'd had a thirty-mile drive ahead of him, he had drunk tonic water all evening, whereas Elizabeth had had several glasses of wine. She wasn't fit, he'd said coldly, expecting her to get out of the driving seat, but instead she'd started the engine, and he'd had no doubt she'd intended to leave him behind in the car park of the hotel.

He remembered grabbing the passenger door and jumping in beside her. The alternative would have been to let her drive off, leaving him to have to explain his plight to those who had still not emerged from the hotel.

It had been at a notorious bend in the road that the car had appeared to go out of control. Jared's stomach still roiled at the memory of jarring gears and squealing tyres, and the horrifying image of an enormous truck bearing down on them. He'd wondered since then whether Elizabeth hadn't had some crazy notion of killing herself and him, but he'd grabbed the wheel out of her hands and wrenched the car back from imminent disaster. Nevertheless it had lost too much traction, and he'd felt the wheels skidding over an icy patch on the road. There'd been no way to prevent the vehicle from mounting the kerb before it had lurched headlong into a ditch.

He didn't recall much after that, until he'd woken up in hospital the following day with two broken legs and a mild concussion. Howard had been sitting by his bed when he'd awakened, and for a moment he'd been sure the older man was there to break the news that Elizabeth was dead.

But Elizabeth hadn't been dead. Though she had been badly injured. Howard's reasons for keeping vigil by his son-in-law's bedside, however, had been to ensure that Jared would take the blame for the accident. Though he hadn't been sure then who had been at the wheel at the time of the crash—they'd both been flung out on impact— he'd wanted to protect his daughter's reputation. And the reputation of the firm, Jared had added silently. If Elizabeth had had to face charges of dangerous driving as well as having been drunk at the wheel, it would have proved a juicy piece of gossip for the press.

Besides, he'd added earnestly, Jared had nothing to lose.

Of course, that hadn't been true, as he'd found out later, when the consequences of the cover-up Howard had engineered had come to light. In addition to her injuries, it appeared that Elizabeth didn't remember anything about the accident, or about the evening, for that matter, and when those injuries had proved to be far more serious than anyone had expected, she'd blamed Jared for causing the paralysis that she was going to have to live with for the rest of her life.

Looking back now, Jared supposed he could have denied everything, but he'd given Howard his word and the old man still knew nothing of what had been going on. Short of destroying the old man emotionally, there was nothing he could have done, at least not then, and as Elizabeth had been going to be in hospital for some time, Jared had decided to wait.

In the three years since that night, Jared's life had, effectively, been put on hold. It had been a very sombre Elizabeth who'd eventually returned home from the hospital, and for a long time after that the house had been filled with nurses and doctors and other members of the

medical profession so that any kind of normal routine had
been impossible.

Howard had arranged for building work to be done to
modify the house for Elizabeth's wheelchair. All doorways
had been widened, and anything she used had been lowered accordingly. He'd even had a lift installed to give her
access to the upper floors of the house, but if he'd ever
suspected that things between his daughter and son-in-law
were not as they should be, he'd kept it to himself.

By the time he'd been able to go home without en-
countering strangers in the house, Jared had shelved his
own ambitions. Although he'd sometimes been tempted to
confront Elizabeth with the truth about the accident, he
never had. In many ways, their relationship had improved
since the accident. Although she was still moody, particularly when things got frustrating for her, Howard had
succeeded in convincing her that there was no way Jared
could be held responsible for what had happened. The road
had been icy; the car had skidded. It was a tragedy, but
no one was to blame.

And Elizabeth knew she had Jared to thank for pro-
tecting her from her father's wrath. The abortion, and its
aftermath, had had to take second place to the injuries
she'd suffered, and even after all this time he had never
betrayed her.

Jared suspected the improvement in their association
was due to two things: one, they no longer made any pretence that theirs was a normal marriage, and, two, the live-
in physiotherapist Howard had hired for her. Although
Jared found Janet Brady too abrasive for his liking, there
was no doubt she had the knack of keeping Elizabeth
sweet.

Howard had also made Jared his deputy at Goldman
Lewis, proving to outsiders, too, that he didn't harbour any
grudges against his son-in-law. The irony of this was not

lost on either of them, but Jared had become an expert at keeping his real feelings to himself.

His relationship with Isobel was not like any other. Meeting her had taught him to despise himself for the man he'd become. He'd realised that the feelings he'd had for Elizabeth were nothing like the way he felt about Isobel. He didn't know if it was love, but he couldn't bear the thought of never seeing her again. Of course he couldn't tell Isobel the truth about the crash without involving Howard. Although he had admitted that he and Elizabeth had been having difficulties long before the accident had occurred, he was loath to betray Howard's confidence when he didn't honestly know how Isobel felt.

He sighed, raking back the tumbled weight of his hair with a restless hand, forcefully closing his mind to what might have been. He had the evening ahead to face, and, unless he wanted to spend the next few hours torturing himself, he had to stop thinking of Isobel and put his own desires aside. But before she'd come along, he'd believed himself immune from any emotional attraction. He hadn't got a divorce because he'd had no intention of ever getting married again. Never wanted to—until now...

The house Howard had given them as a wedding present four years ago was situated in an exclusive development north-west of the city, and Jared contained his impatience as he joined the usual rush-hour press of traffic heading in that direction. As he waited at one of the numerous sets of traffic lights, he contemplated calling Isobel and asking her what she was doing this evening, but the knowledge of how he would feel if she told him she was free stopped him from picking up his mobile phone.

There was no way he could see her tonight, and he closed his eyes for a moment as the image of making love with her in her mother's kitchen of all places flashed across his mind. God, he thought, remembering that afternoon with sudden incredulity, anyone could have looked through the window and seen them there. All the doors had been unlocked. How would he have felt if that snobby sister of hers had walked in and found them?

The lights changed and he allowed the car to crawl forward to the next obstruction. The trouble was, when he was with Isobel such considerations went out the window, and he wondered if he wasn't in danger of not giving a damn...

He parked on the brick-paved forecourt in front of the triple garage which was situated to one side of the sprawling pseudo-mansion he'd learned to call home. It had never been his choice; he would have preferred something older. But appearances mattered to Elizabeth and this house said that they'd made it in the material world.

Gathering up his jacket, his briefcase, and his mobile phone, Jared pushed open the door and got out of the car. But he'd forgotten a portfolio of drawings that he'd brought from the current development, and by the time he'd rescued it from the back seat his hands were full.

He kicked the door closed with his foot, his lips twisting at the thought of treating a car he'd used to dream about when he was a teenager so shabbily. Then he saw Janet Brady watching him from Elizabeth's bedroom window, and all humour went of the situation. She was probably thinking he was venting his frustration on the vehicle, and he was. But it wasn't just the prospect of another formal dinner party that was souring his mood.

He heard the whine of the lift Howard had installed as soon as he entered the marble-tiled hallway. The ornamental cage came to a halt as Jared was shouldering the outer door closed behind him, and the wheelchair came gliding towards him.

'Did you get it?'

Elizabeth's first words were interrogative, and for a moment Jared couldn't think what on earth she meant. His own thoughts were still wrapped up with what he had been thinking on the drive home, and he looked at his wife without comprehension as she gazed up at him with enquiring eyes.

'Get what?' he asked, unloading the file and the briefcase onto the hall table, and her lips curled impatiently at any hint of opposition.

'The watch,' she exclaimed tersely, tucking a blonde strand behind her ear. 'Did you pick it up from the engraver's? Oh, don't tell me you forgot it, Jared. Temple's will be closed by now.'

Jared laid his mobile phone beside the portfolio, and bent to flick the catches on the briefcase. 'Oh, that,' he said carelessly, extracting a box from inside. He turned and handed it to her. 'I'm not entirely without sensitivity, you know.'

Elizabeth didn't bother to answer him. Her attention was focussed on the cardboard-covered leather case he'd handed her, and Jared was able to observe her without restraint. She was still a beautiful woman, though in recent years she'd gained some weight, but her features still possessed a certain sharpness even if her body was plumper than it used to be.

She slid the covering from the case now and opened it to gaze at the pocket watch that lay inside. It was a gold half-hunter, gleaming brightly on its bed of white satin, and Elizabeth picked it up and turned it over, smiling with satisfaction when she read the inscription on the back.

'"To Daddy on his sixtieth birthday,"' she murmured, the pad of her thumb rubbing the engraving as she spoke. '"With all my love."'

Jared winced. He doubted Elizabeth had it in her to love anyone. 'Is that what you had put on the back?' he asked tightly, and his wife looked up at him with scornful eyes.

Then, her own lips tightening with unwilling pique, she handed the watch to him and he saw the inscription for himself. '"With all *our* love,"' he read, '"Liza and Jared". Very nice.'

'It should be,' exclaimed Elizabeth, putting the watch back in its case. 'It cost plenty. I just hope it's enough.'

A headache was probing at Jared's temple, but her words demanded an explanation. 'Enough?' he echoed. 'Enough for what?'

Elizabeth shrugged. 'To distract him from his usual theme, of course,' she declared, as if Jared should have known what she was talking about. 'You know how irritating he's been lately.'

'Has he?'

Jared hadn't noticed any change in his father-in-law's attitude towards him, but Elizabeth's nostrils flared with evident impatience. 'Well, naturally, I wouldn't expect you to notice,' she said bitterly. 'You probably think that the fact that he's become such bosom buddies with Patrick Beaumont lately is just a coincidence.'

Jared sighed. 'Does it matter?'

'It matters to me.' Elizabeth twisted her hands together. 'Jared, Patrick's a consultant gynaecologist. Surely even you must know what Daddy's thinking.'

Jared began to understand. 'You're afraid he's going to bring up the possibility of you having a baby,' he said flatly. 'Well, you've got to tell him the truth sooner or later.'

'I can't.'

Jared shrugged. 'Just don't expect me to do it.'

Elizabeth bit her lip. 'You could tell him that in your opinion you don't think I could cope with a baby. That it wouldn't be fair on me to insist on my having a lot of unnecessary tests.'

Jared's mouth was grim. 'You have to be joking.' He would have brushed past her then, if she hadn't swung her chair and blocked his path. 'Dammit, Liz, you got rid of my child and, in the process, any chance you ever had of having another baby. Don't expect me to help you when you haven't even got the guts to tell your father yourself.'

Elizabeth's mouth compressed. 'Let's not forget that if it wasn't for you I wouldn't be in this wheelchair,' she said accusingly, and Jared had to bite his tongue to prevent himself from telling her the truth.

He pushed the chair aside and strode towards the stairs. He was making no promises to her when the only thing he really wanted was out of his reach. 'I need a shower,' he said, without giving her an answer, and vaulted up the stairs to the first floor.

He met Janet Brady on the landing. She was a tall woman, almost as tall as he was, with coarse red hair that she wore plaited in a single braid. She was overweight, too, and was invariably dressed in trousers with a loose blouse to hide her waistband, and the look she cast in Jared's direction was loaded with dislike.

'I should have thought you'd know better than to upset your wife, Mr Kendall,' she said sharply. 'Her therapy isn't just a physical thing, you know.'

'When I want your advice, Miss Brady, I'll ask for it,' retorted Jared, striding down the corridor to his bedroom, and it wasn't until he'd slammed the door behind him that he realised she must have been listening to everything he and Elizabeth had said.

CHAPTER FIVE

THE cottage stood at the end of a row of similar dwellings, but, unlike the others, it had been sadly neglected. A drooping gate gave onto a front garden that was choked with weeds, and the flagged path was covered with moss.

'You'll have to be careful you don't slip when it's wet,' Michelle remarked, following her friend though the gate. 'God, I hope the inside is better than this.'

Isobel was thinking the same, but she refused to be downhearted about it. She had so much else to be downhearted about, and finding this cottage had seemed the only bright spot in a rather dull day. When the estate agent in Polgarth had told her that there was a cottage to rent in Polgarron, she'd fairly jumped at the chance of finding a home so near to Tregarth Hall. But it was only now, when they came to inspect it, that they realised why the estate agent had been so willing to trust them with the key.

There were roses climbing over the porch, but she felt the unpleasant brush of spiders' webs as she stepped forward and put the key in the lock. It was obviously weeks, possibly even months, since anyone had visited here, and her heart sank a little when she had to apply her shoulder to open the door.

'Damp,' said Michelle resignedly, stepping inside and giving an involuntary shiver. 'Issy, you can't stay here. It's uninhabitable.'

Isobel put her own misgivings aside and looked about her with determined optimism. 'You're too pessimistic,' she said. 'And you've got soft, living in the lap of luxury as you do.'

'Issy, a three-bedroomed semi is not the lap of luxury.

Admit it: this isn't what you expected. No wonder that smarmy devil in the estate agent's was so eager to pass you the key. He probably thinks we're thick or something. I mean, no one in their right mind would rent this place.'

'We haven't seen it yet,' Isobel insisted, but she conceded to herself that the dismal room they were standing in would need more than soap and water to put it right. The windows were thick with dirt, but that didn't prevent them from seeing that the paper on the walls was peeling, and no one had touched the paintwork in heaven knew how many years.

'What's to see?' Michelle countered now, walking across the stained linoleum that covered the floor. She pushed open the door into the adjoining room, brushing away the cobwebs before venturing further. 'God, this must be the kitchen! Issy, have you ever seen anything like this?'

Isobel hadn't. She wasn't averse to primitive, but when it came to using a pump to get any water, cold or otherwise, she realised she had to draw the line. Besides which, there was no sign of any electrical appliances; not even a cooker.

'It is pretty—pretty—'

'I think the word you're looking for is ghastly,' declared Michelle fervently, backing out of the kitchen and turning away. 'Come on, Issy. Let's go and tell that estate agent what we think of him. I think we've got time before they close for the day.'

Isobel sighed, and as she did so a shadow further darkened the doorway behind them. A man had appeared in the entrance, and both women took a step backward as he came into the room.

'Can I help you?' he asked, and an errant ray of sunlight that had found its way between the smears of dirt on the windows highlighted reddish brown hair and a square, good-looking face.

Isobel glanced at Michelle, but her friend only arched a quizzical brow and she realised it was up to her to answer him. 'Um—I doubt it,' she said, wondering if he was another prospective tenant the agency had sent along. 'We were just leaving.'

'Really?' The man, who she could see now was somewhere in his late twenties, looked disappointed. 'I was hoping you might be interested in taking this place on.'

Isobel blinked. 'You were?' She frowned. 'Why should it matter to you?'

'Oh, forgive me.' The man, who was dressed in brown corduroy pants, a Barbour jacket and green boots, stepped forward, holding out his hand. 'I haven't introduced myself, have I? I'm Luke Herrington. My family owns this cottage, I'm afraid.'

And all the others as well, thought Isobel sagely, allowing him to shake her hand. 'How do you do? I'm Isobel D—Dawson.' She exchanged an appealing look with Michelle, begging her condolence. 'And this is my friend, Michelle Chambers.'

There were handshakes all round, but it was obvious that Luke Herrington was more interested in Isobel's dark slenderness than Michelle's more generous proportions. 'And am I right in thinking that the agency in Polgarth sent you here?' he asked, pulling a wry face, and Isobel nodded.

'Yes. But I'm afraid it's not what—what we're looking for.'

'Because of the state it's in, I'll bet,' agreed Luke Herrington warmly. 'I must admit, I hadn't realised just how dilapidated it had become.'

'It's a dump,' said Michelle flatly. 'I don't know how anyone could have expected us to take it.'

'Oh, I agree.' Herrington nodded his head vigorously. 'I'd never have allowed Gillings to send anybody here if I'd known.'

Both women took that with a pinch of salt, but the man's next words gave them pause. 'Of course, if you were interested, I'd be happy to have the place renovated for you. I mean,' he pressed on, when it appeared possible that at least one of the women was listening to him, 'no one wants to leave a property standing empty for months on end. Particularly not when a few rolls of paper and a few pots of paint could make it habitable.'

'Oh, I think it would take more than that,' said Michelle disparagingly, ignoring Isobel's reaction. 'The kitchen doesn't even have running water.'

'Oh, I'm sure it does.' Luke Herrington frowned now. 'Let me see...'

But when Michelle turned back towards the open doorway, he stopped her. 'That's not the kitchen,' he said, and Isobel didn't know whether to be glad or sorry. 'That's just a storeroom. The kitchen's this way.'

He led them out of another door into a narrow passageway that ran towards the back of the cottage. The kitchen was the only door opening off the hall, with a narrow flight of stairs curving towards the upper floor opposite.

'Here we are,' he said, dipping his head under the low lintel. 'What do you think?'

The kitchen was tiny, but he was right, it did have running hot and cold water—or it would have if the boiler was working—and there was a small gas cooker and electric fridge.

'It's—antique,' declared Michelle, before Isobel could find some polite adjective to use, and just for a moment a look of irritation crossed Herrington's handsome face.

'It's—primitive, I'll give you that,' he said, running the tip of one finger along the rim of the fridge and then grimacing at the smear of dirt it left behind. 'But, as I say, it could be made quite—comfortable.'

'And how long do you think that would take?' asked Isobel, wondering if she was mad to be even thinking of living here. She'd already given him a false surname, and she was glad that Michelle had given her name and address as a guarantee when the estate agent had handed over the key.

'Oh—let me see.' Herrington glanced about him. 'Two or three weeks, I suppose.'

'Two or three months, more like,' muttered Michelle, making her opinion very plain, and once again he gave her an impatient look.

'Will you be living here, too, Miss Chambers?' he asked politely, and Isobel guessed that Gillings had phoned and told him that only one of them was looking for accommodation.

'It's *Mrs* Chambers,' replied Michelle coldly. 'And, no, I won't be living here. But I think Issy should think again about where she wants to live.'

Taking a deep breath, Herrington turned back to Isobel. 'Do you have some connection with this area, Miss Dawson?' he asked, and for a moment Isobel wondered if he'd detected that she had some ulterior motive for choosing Polgarron. But then, realising he was only making conversation, she shook her head.

'I was just looking for somewhere to rent in this area,' she admitted. 'This cottage was vacant, so...'

She shrugged, and he inclined his head. 'I see.' He gestured that they should move out into the hall again. 'Come, let me show you upstairs.'

There were two bedrooms, and a minuscule bathroom that contained a suite that, like the kitchen downstairs, had seen better days. But the bedrooms themselves were considerably less off-putting, the view from the windows making up in no small part for what they lacked in size.

'What do you think?'

Herrington was looking at her now, and Isobel didn't know what to say. The cottage wasn't really what she was looking for. It was small, even by her standards, and there was no central heating, which she'd told herself she had to have for when the baby was born.

'I'm not sure...' she said awkwardly, and Michelle took the opportunity to endorse her own feelings.

'You need somewhere more modern, Issy,' she exclaimed. 'An apartment would be better than this.'

With a baby? Isobel didn't say the words but the thought passed between them, and she had to admit that although having a baby in an apartment wasn't ideal, it was gaining more merit. After all, this wasn't the first house they'd been offered, but all of them had had something wrong with them, most usually the rent.

'I don't know...'

She was loath to dismiss the cottage out of hand. Despite its bedraggled appearance, she tended to agree with Luke Herrington; it could be made habitable, and not too expensively. Besides which, she'd never had a garden of her own before, and she could already see a lawn and a rose garden, and a pram standing in the sunshine beside the door...

'Let me get my bailiff to take a look at it,' said Luke eagerly, sensing her reluctance to turn him down. 'Are you staying locally? Let me get him to give you an estimate of how long it will take to put the place in order.'

'Oh, I—'

'I've got to do something about this place anyway,' he persisted. 'As I said before, if I'd realised just how run-down it had become, I'd have done something about it before now.'

Isobel looked at Michelle for guidance, but her friend was saying nothing more. Isobel knew what she was thinking without having to be told, but the knowledge that she might have to spend another week trailing round unsuitable properties was urging her to at least give Luke a chance.

'We're staying in Polgarth,' she said, making a decision. 'At the White Hart. Do you know it?'

'Indeed I do.' Luke beamed now. 'Frank Culver, the landlord, you know, is a good friend of mine. I'm sure he's making you very comfortable there.'

'Better than here,' said Michelle under her breath, but Isobel heard her.

'We're very comfortable,' she said, hoping her would-be landlord hadn't heard Michelle's comment. 'All right. I suggest I leave it for the time being. I'll keep looking round, and you can let me know when your bailiff has had the chance to give his assessment.'

'Excellent.' Clearly, he was looking forward to having her as his tenant, and Isobel hoped he would feel just as enthusiastic when he realised she wasn't going to be entirely alone at the cottage.

But, back in the car again, Michelle let her feel the brunt of her frustration. 'I can't believe you're going to consider that dump,' she exclaimed, accelerating through the village in an effort to expunge her irritation. 'For God's sake, Issy, I know you want to find somewhere to live and we haven't been having a great deal of success lately, but—'

'We only have another week,' Isobel reminded her desperately. 'Then you'll be going back to Newcastle, and I'll have to go looking at places on foot. Unless I get someone to deliver my car. Not to mention the fact that I'd rather not go alone.'

'But you don't want my opinion,' Michelle pointed out shortly. 'I couldn't believe it when you told that ass where we were staying. You as good as accepted his offer there and then.'

'No, I didn't.' Isobel sighed. 'Oh, Michelle, don't be angry with me, please. You know how much I want to live in this area. What are the chances of us finding anywhere else to rent that's as convenient as this?'

'Pretty slim, I suppose,' Michelle conceded, opening her

window and resting her arm on the sill. 'And this is a pretty village, I suppose. I like all the grey stonework, and that church looks interesting.'

'Hmm.' Isobel squeezed Michelle's arm with grateful fingers. 'Thanks.'

Then, her eyes widened. 'My God!'

'What? What?' Michelle grabbed the wheel with both hands, nearly steering off the road in her efforts to control the car.

'There. *There!*' said Isobel, pointing a shaking finger. 'That sign; can you see it? It says, "Tregarth Hall"! Oh, God, Michelle, that must be where those letters came from.'

Michelle left for home six days later.

She was loath to leave her friend, still staying at the inn in Polgarth, but it was a long journey back to Newcastle and she and her husband were leaving for Portugal in a few days.

'What do I say to Marion, if I see her?' she asked, as she and Isobel lingered over dinner the night before she left. So far, all Isobel's sister knew was that she and Michelle were holidaying together, but sooner or later Marion would have to be given a proper explanation.

Even so, Isobel was loath to tell her about the baby just in case Marion happened to mention it to someone at the golf club. The idea that Jared might find out via some crony of Howard Goldman's was unacceptable, but Michelle wasn't convinced that she should keep it a secret from her family.

'If you have to, tell her I've decided to prolong my holiday,' Isobel said now, avoiding the other woman's eyes. 'There's another four weeks before term's due to start. It'll be easier if I'm settled into the cottage before I tell her and Malcolm I'm not coming back.'

Michelle sighed. 'I still think you should have been

straight with her. About moving, at least. Whether you tell her about the baby is up to you, but I think she deserves to know that you've resigned from your job.'

'I know.' Isobel pulled a wry face. 'But you know why I didn't.'

'Of course. Because you were afraid someone else would find out. But he didn't and you're here now. What have you got to lose?'

Isobel shrugged. 'Nothing, I suppose.' But the knowledge of how Jared would react when he discovered what she'd done was tearing her apart, and she knew it was foolish but, so long as she didn't tell anyone else, she could fool herself into believing that it wasn't a final break.

It had been so hard not seeing him again before she left. She hadn't been able to avoid speaking to him on the phone, of course, but she'd managed to find excuses for not meeting him in the two weeks after his visit to her mother's house. After that scene, and its aftermath, she'd known she couldn't see him again. She was too weak, too vulnerable; he only had to lay his hands on her and she went to pieces.

God knew what he was thinking of her now. He'd have called the apartment and discovered that her number had been discontinued, but would he have been indiscreet enough to ask Marion where she was? He knew her sister had found out about their relationship, but he also knew that Isobel had told him that it was over, and that she had probably told Marion the same thing, so...

'So does that mean that if she asks I can tell her where you are?' Michelle persisted now, and, forcing thoughts of Jared to the back of her mind, Isobel took a deep breath.

'I'm not sure—'

'But you can't expect her to believe that I don't know where you are,' said Michelle impatiently. 'Issy, accept it.

You've made the break. Kendall's going to have to live with it.'

'I know.'

'I'm not sure you do.' Michelle looked worried now. 'Dammit, I wish I didn't have to go back.'

'But you do,' said Isobel, finishing the mineral water in her glass. She forced a smile. 'I'll be all right. Honestly. I'm not a complete fool, you know.'

'Remember, you've got to check in with a doctor at the first possible moment. And make arrangements about— well, about when the baby's due.'

'I know.'

'The provisional date you have is January eighteenth, isn't it?'

'You know it is.'

'I wonder if that coincides with a weekend?' Michelle bit her lip. 'Perhaps I could get a flight to Penzance or somewhere. It would be so much quicker than bringing the car, and if the weather's bad—'

'Michelle.' Isobel reached across the table and covered her friend's hand with her own. 'I don't expect you to be here when I have the baby.'

'But someone has to be.'

'Not necessarily.'

Isobel suppressed the panicky little feeling that assailed her at the thought of going into labour at the cottage and having to drive herself to the hospital in—where? She didn't even know where the nearest hospital was. Polgarth was the nearest small town, but not all small towns had maternity units. She might have to go to Truro or St Austell. God, how far away was that?

A little of her anxiety must have shown in her face, because Michelle gripped her fingers now. 'What is it? What are you thinking? Issy, I'll try to be here. I will.'

Isobel shook her head. 'I'm just being silly.' She made

herself give a short laugh. 'I was thinking, I don't even know where the nearest hospital is.'

'Well, at least you'll have plenty of time to find out before it happens,' Michelle reassured her. 'And I'll be down again in the October break.'

'Phil's going to get sick of you leaving him on his own,' said Isobel at once. 'There's no need—'

'Hey, Phil may come with me,' Michelle interrupted her quickly. 'He gets more than two weeks' holiday a year, you know.'

Isobel's eyes widened. 'Do you think he would? Come, I mean?'

'Why not?' Michelle grinned. 'So if you find you've got any little jobs that need doing, just leave them to him.'

Isobel's smile was tearful. 'What would I do without you?'

'You'd manage.' Michelle was philosophical. 'I dare say that if Herrington has anything to do with it, you won't be on your own for long.'

'Until he finds out I'm expecting another man's child,' remarked Isobel drily.

'Well…' Michelle shrugged. 'He wasn't the reason you decided to take the cottage, was he?'

'No.' Isobel was thoughtful. 'I wonder if he is still alive. My father, I mean. It's going to be interesting finding out.'

'Well, be careful,' said Michelle warningly. 'Don't forget, his wife may still be alive, and he may not want to acknowledge something he's spent the last twenty-five—twenty-six years trying to forget.'

Isobel nodded. 'I realise that. And I'm not planning on doing anything rash. But—I would like to see him. You can understand that?'

Michelle regarded her gently. 'I understand,' she assured her. 'I just wish I could stay around to see it.'

CHAPTER SIX

JARED gazed at the plans for the new Hermitage shopping complex and leisure centre without really seeing them. He'd had this particular set of drawings on his desk for the past week, and, although he knew he had to have them ready to present to the board of Hermitage Developments in a few days, he couldn't seem to concentrate on anything at present.

No matter how he tried to apply himself, the knowledge that Isobel had apparently disappeared gnawed like a continuous pain in his gut. If he managed to divert himself for a few minutes, it didn't last: some action, some memory, bringing it all back into painful focus.

He couldn't believe she'd done this to him. Oh, he knew what she'd said the last time they'd been together, but she'd tried to finish with him before and it had never worked. They needed one another; they enjoyed being together too much to allow anyone to come between them. Or so he'd thought. How the hell was he supposed to know what she was thinking now?

He stifled a groan.

He supposed that was what was crippling him most: the knowledge that she had indeed left town without even telling him she was going, let alone where. She'd closed up her apartment, had her phone disconnected, and then simply disappeared. And there was no one he could turn to for information.

How could she do that? How could she abandon him without a word of explanation? He'd even tried to find that friend of hers, Michelle Chambers, but she was apparently away, too. Were they together? Was it just a prolonged holiday? Or did she really have something more permanent in mind?

Everything he'd been able to find out for himself pointed to the latter. Her apartment was empty. Jared had managed to use his contacts to speak to the landlord on the pretext of looking for an apartment for someone else. He'd confirmed that Isobel had cancelled her lease before she left. The phone was another obvious give-away. No one had their phone disconnected for just a couple of weeks.

So where had she gone? *Why* had she gone? And, please God, was she ever coming back?

The opening of his office door curtailed any further introspection. Howard Goldman came into the room, brandishing a sheaf of contracts that he wanted Jared to have a look at before they were signed. 'You're not still working on those drawings?' the older man asked, coming round the desk to peer over his son-in-law's shoulder. 'Dammit, Jared, they're coming on Friday. I don't want any last-minute hitches to hold up this deal.'

'There won't be.' Jared wished he could feel as sure as he sounded. 'I'm just having a bad day, that's all.'

Howard frowned, drawing back to look at him. 'Yes,' he said, after a few moments' study. 'I can see you are. Hell, Jared, you're not sickening for something, are you? I need you on this project. Mercer asked specifically for your participation.'

A thin smile crossed Jared's lips. 'That sounds like a compliment, Howard. Should I be flattered or what?' It was rare that his father-in-law handed out any plaudits, and now he gave the younger man a rueful look.

'You know damn well your designs are appreciated,' he declared gruffly. 'You don't think I'd be giving you the cream of the work that comes in here if I didn't think you were the best man for the job.' He paused, taking a breath. 'But I have to say I've been disappointed in the lack of enthusiasm you've shown over the Hermitage development. What's wrong with you, man? Is Liza making your life difficult? I've told you, I've arranged for us all to go on that cruise in September. You'll enjoy it and we all need a break.'

The cruise!

Jared lay back in his chair as Howard moved round the desk again, and, giving the older man a rueful smile, he said, 'Holidays! Aren't they supposed to be the third most stressful event in your life? After divorce and moving house?'

Howard stared at him. 'You don't want to go?'

Jared straightened his spine. 'I'm not a holiday person, Howard. You should know that.'

Howard's disappointment was evident. 'Does Liza know how you feel?'

'No.' Jared was defensive now. It was bad enough that he couldn't take any satisfaction from his work in his present mood without his father-in-law putting his mistaken interpretation to the facts. 'Besides, I don't think that's relevant. So long as Janet Brady's around, she won't give a damn.'

Howard's expression softened. 'You don't have to swear at me, boy. I'm not your enemy.' He sighed. 'I know Liza can be difficult. Who better? It would be different if she had someone other than that Brady woman to distract her from her own problems. I know she's always going to be paralysed, but that doesn't mean she can't live a normal life.'

Jared stiffened. He could guess what was coming. 'Don't you think she lives a reasonably normal life now?' he asked.

Howard didn't immediately answer him. Instead, he flung himself down into the chair opposite and rolled the sheaf of contracts between his hands. 'I was talking to Pat Beaumont the other day,' he said. 'You know Beaumont, don't you? He works at the County. Hospital, that is. He and I have a similar handicap.' He grimaced. 'I mean on the golf course, of course.'

'So?'

Jared's response was wary, but Howard didn't seem to notice. 'He's a good chap. Used to work at some well-known teaching hospital in London. He knows what he's talking about.' He nodded. 'You can take it from me.'

'A good man to know, then.' Jared was sardonic. 'What is he? A cardiologist? A neurosurgeon?'

'He's a gynaecologist,' exclaimed Howard shortly, looking impatient. 'He's had quite a lot of experience with women in Liza's condition. According to him, there's absolutely no reason why she shouldn't have a baby even now.'

Jared blew out a breath. 'What if she doesn't want a baby?'

Howard's brows ascended. 'What kind of a question is that? Of course she wants a baby. Hasn't she always said how much she wishes she could give me a grandchild?'

Had she? Jared didn't know anything about that, but it was typical of Elizabeth to try and pass the blame.

'I don't think it's practical, in the circumstances,' he declared flatly. 'Our marriage is hardly normal as it is.'

'That's just what I'm saying. Elizabeth needs something to distract her.' Howard snorted. 'Naturally, we'd employ a full-time nanny. But the baby would be ours—yours! What do you say?'

What could he say?

'I think you'd better talk to her about it,' he said, straightening the papers on his desk. There was no way he and Elizabeth could have a child, even if it were possible. He realised he was getting older too, and he wanted his life back.

'But she won't talk to me,' protested his father-in-law frustratedly. 'Not about her condition, anyway. When it comes to discussing the future, she just clams up. You know that. I don't want to upset her, Jared, but I'm not getting any younger.

'You're hardly in your dotage,' said Jared evenly, but Howard was serious.

'I spoke to Dr Hardesty last week,' he admitted heavily. 'I've been having some indigestion lately, and I wanted him to check me out.'

'And?' Jared was concerned.

'Well, he thinks there's nothing wrong. But no one can be sure of their own longevity, and Liza doesn't seem to realise it.'

Jared shook his head, relieved to find it was nothing more serious, and, unwilling to destroy all the old man's hopes so arbitrarily, he blew out a breath. 'I'm sorry,' he said. 'I really must get on with this presentation. Do you think I should concentrate on the overall concept or point out that certain building regulations may limit us on height levels and so on?'

Howard's jaw clamped. 'So you won't talk to her?' He grimaced. 'Oh, well, we'll have plenty of time to discuss it while we're away.' His eyes narrowed. 'Don't let me down, Jared. We need each other too much to let Liza's pig-headedness come between us.'

Jared didn't contradict him. There'd be time enough to marshal his arguments why he couldn't accompany them on the cruise later on. After he'd found Isobel, he reflected tautly. After he'd found her and persuaded her to come back.

Apparently deciding he'd done as much as he could for the present, too, Howard turned to business matters, and by the time he'd left Jared was reasonably sure the old man had put it out of his mind. There was no room for sentiment when it came to business. And his observations were as sharp as ever.

Which was all to the good, thought Jared, taking off his

glasses. Then, after massaging his lids with his finger and thumb, he replaced them again. And, ironically enough, he worked better for the rest of the afternoon. Howard's comments had caused him to take an unbiased look at himself. Perhaps it was time to take a harder look at his life.

He phoned Marion Rimmer later that evening.

He'd met Isobel's sister a couple of times, at charity events and the like, but this was the first time he'd spoken to her personally. Isobel had told him she'd found out about their relationship, so he had no fears that he was betraying her confidence. But he was also aware that Marion resented him, though he never could decide whether it was because he was deceiving Elizabeth or because he was doing it with her sister.

A young girl's voice answered the phone. Emily, he guessed. Isobel had told him her niece's name, but he knew better than to appear too familiar with the child.

'Is your mother there?' he asked, and with the innocent honesty of youth Emily went to get her.

'Who is it?' He could hear Isobel's sister chiding her daughter in the background, and then, having received an unsatisfactory reply, Marion herself came on the line. 'Hello? Marion Rimmer speaking.'

'Um—Mrs Rimmer.' Now that he had her undivided attention, Jared felt briefly stunned at his audacity. And then, before she could begin to think it was a crank call, he added, 'This is Jared Kendall.'

There was a silence that was almost palpably chilly, and then Marion seemed to remember he was related to the Goldmans, and recovered her composure. 'Mr Kendall,' she said, with cool politeness. 'How can I help you?'

Jared dragged his lower lip between his teeth and bit down hard. Then, steeling himself for her response, he said evenly, 'I wonder if you could tell me when Isobel will be back.'

'Isobel!' The woman repeated her sister's name with evident irritation. 'I'd have thought you'd know that better than me, Mr Kendall.'

'Well, I don't.' Jared couldn't prevent the harsh rejoinder. But getting angry with Marion wasn't going to solve anything, and, calming himself again, he continued, 'I thought you might have a forwarding address.'

'A forwarding address?' If he hadn't known better, he'd have sworn that Marion's reaction was as blank as his had been. 'People who go on a touring holiday don't leave a forwarding address, Mr Kendall. And now, if you—'

'She hasn't gone on a holiday,' put in Jared quickly, revising his earlier opinion of her understanding. 'Her apartment's empty.'

There was another silence, a shorter one this time, and then Marion said faintly, 'What do you mean, her apartment's empty? Of course it is. I've told you: she's away.'

'She's cancelled the lease,' Jared told her flatly, his heart sinking at the news that her family was as much in the dark as he was. 'I don't think she's coming back.'

'Oh, no. No. You must be mistaken.' He was relieved to hear anxiety in her voice now. However disapproving she might be of him, she still cared about her sister, and it must be worrying to realise that Isobel had left without telling anyone where she was going and what she planned to do. 'She'd have said something, given me some inkling—'

'And she didn't?'

'No. No.' He heard her swallow rather convulsively. 'Unless—unless this has something to do with those letters.'

'Letters?'

Jared's senses were alert to any clue that might explain Isobel's disappearance, and although he was sure that at any other time Marion would have bitten her tongue out rather than give him any information, she was still in a state of shock and she'd briefly forgotten who she was talking to.

'Those letters from her father,' she said, almost unthinkingly. 'Surely she told you about them? You knew she was adopted, didn't you?'

Jared's fingers were in danger of crushing the receiver. 'Oh—those letters,' he said, as if he knew all about them. 'I'd—forgotten about them. Do you think they're relevant?'

'Yes.' Marion was obviously still trying to put two and two together. 'She knew I didn't approve of her tampering with the past, of course. I mean, if her real father had wanted to meet her—' She broke off, and then went on more thoughtfully, 'Oh, where was that place they were from? Tregarth or Tregarron or something.'

Jared hardly dared to breathe for fear of diverting her. 'I'm not sure,' he said, his mind already working on a plan that would give him a few days to find out. 'But— you think she might have gone to find her father?' He was feeling his way blindly now. 'Is that likely?'

'Well, it's possible.' But Marion was recovering her composure. He could hear it in her voice. 'Not that it's any business of yours.'

Jared's smile was bitter. 'No.'

'And if she'd wanted you to know where she was going, she'd have told you,' she continued, and Jared had to suppress a very real urge to say the same was true for her.

But he didn't. When Marion cut the call short, he put the phone down with the first real feeling of optimism he'd had for weeks. It wasn't much, but he had a name. Well, two names, actually. And, as he'd never heard of either of them, he thought it was a safe bet that they weren't large municipalities. Most likely they were small towns or villages, and surely someone, a hotel receptionist, an estate agent, somebody, would remember a woman as unfamiliar—as beautiful—as Isobel.

If only Marion had mentioned the father's name…

CHAPTER SEVEN

ISOBEL moved into the cottage four weeks later.

She wouldn't have believed that so much could be accomplished in so short a period of time, but Luke Herrington had kept his word and the transformation of Raven Cottage from its previously run-down state was quite remarkable.

To begin with, the whole place had been cleaned and redecorated. The chimneys had been swept and fires lighted, and modern appliances had replaced the ancient fixtures in the kitchen. The bathroom fitments were the original ones, but Isobel had been enchanted to discover that beneath the dirt and grime the cast-iron bath and basin were as pure and unstained as any she'd seen in specialist catalogues that catered to people's tastes for Victoriana.

She'd visited the cottage several times during the renovations, trying to work out where she was going to put her furniture when it arrived. It had been put in storage before she and Michelle left Newcastle, and she was looking forward to having her own things around her again. She missed having a radio, and her own bed, and she got quite excited at the thought of having a whole house at her disposal. Apart from when she'd lived at home, she'd been confined to the apartment, and two bedrooms, a bath and kitchen/diner, all on one floor, were not as spacious as this.

Most of the men who had worked at the cottage were local, but although Isobel had tried to strike up a conversation with them they hadn't been very forthcoming. It could have been because they were very conscientious about getting their work done, but Isobel suspected it was more personal than that. She'd noticed a certain stand-offishness about most of the people in the village, and she guessed they were suspicious of her reasons for being there.

She could hardly blame them. From what she'd gathered from the landlord at the White Hart in Polgarth, strangers were few and far between in Polgarron, and they were probably curious as to why someone young and apparently unattached like herself should choose to move from one end of the country to the other.

Of course, she hadn't gone into her reasons with the landlord. No matter how tempting it would have been to ask if he knew the owner of Tregarth Hall, she'd contained her impatience, contenting herself with ringing directory enquiries and affirming that there were indeed Dorlands still living there. The number was ex-directory, as she'd half expected, and she still had no clear idea how—or even if—she was going to try and contact her father. For the present, it was enough to know that he was there.

On a more practical note, she'd contacted the local education authorities and had her name put on the supply list for the new term. At present, they could give her no information as to possible placements, but once the new term was underway they would have a better idea of future vacancies.

She'd also had her car transported from Newcastle to Polgarth. After speaking to Michelle when she got back from Portugal, and discovering that Jared had been seen visiting the apartments where she used to live, she'd decided it would probably be wiser to contact a local garage in Cornwall and have them effect the transfer. Dealing with a garage in Newcastle would leave too many loose ends, and she didn't trust Jared not to use any means to try and find her.

That was why, when she eventually gave her new address to Marion, she intended to ask her not to discuss it with anyone. Although she didn't expect Jared would be reckless enough to contact her sister direct, word could get around and she wanted to cut it off at source. She knew Michelle was totally trustworthy. Her friend wouldn't betray her whereabouts, and there was no one else.

She had encountered Luke Herrington at the cottage just two days before she was due to move in. His bailiff had given her the keys the day before, and as her furniture was being delivered the following day, she'd decided to do some preliminary shopping and fill the fridge.

She'd been unpacking a few personal belongings she'd brought with her from the inn in Polgarth when she had heard the sound of a car outside. On the off-chance that she might have to take a furnished apartment, Michelle had suggested she bring such things as books and ornaments, towels and linens, away with her, which was why the Chambers' estate car had been so much more useful than Isobel's small saloon when they'd first driven down here. Ever since then they'd been stored in a pile of boxes in the corner of her room at the White Hart, and she'd realised it would take more than just one trip to transport them to the cottage.

However, when she'd heard the sudden cessation of the car's engine, her hands had stilled over the box of books she'd been stowing on some fitted shelves beside the fireplace in the living room. Her mouth had gone dry, and a nervous quiver had gripped her stomach, and for a heartstopping moment she had wondered if Jared could have found her after all. But then common sense had overcome her involuntary panic, and, smoothing her hands over the seat of her black leggings, she had gone to meet her visitor.

'Oh—Mr Herrington,' she said, not without some relief, when she opened the door. He'd knocked as she was heading for the door, but she'd deliberately steeled herself not to look out of the window like some frightened rabbit. 'Um—won't you come in?'

'Thank you.' He stepped immediately into the newly decorated living room, glancing about him with some satisfaction at the gleaming white paintwork and subtly patterned walls. 'Well, this looks much better,' he remarked pleasantly. 'Does it meet with your approval?'

Isobel smiled. 'Very much,' she said. Then, seeing his glance move to the box of books, 'I was just making a start at moving in.'

'I can see that.' He strolled casually across the room and rescued a copy of *Pride and Prejudice* from the floor. 'Ah, Jane Austen.' He smiled. 'Are you a romantic, Miss Dawson?'

Isobel took a deep breath. 'It's—it's not Dawson,' she said, coming to a decision. 'It's Dorland, actually. I—didn't like to correct you before.'

Luke's reddish-gold brows drew together in some confusion. 'Oh, but—' He put the book down and pulled a rent book from his pocket. 'I was about to give you this.' He grimaced. 'I'll have to change the name.'

'Yes.' Isobel twisted her hands together at her waist, feeling awful for having deceived him. 'It was an easy mistake to make.'

'I suppose so.' He frowned. 'Dorland. That's quite an unusual name, isn't it? Did you know there are Dorlands living in the village?'

'No!' Isobel hoped she didn't look as guilty as she felt. 'How interesting.' She hesitated. 'Not such an unusual name, after all, then.'

'Perhaps not.' Luke frowned. 'Where was it you said you came from? Newark? Newmarket?'

'Newcastle,' said Isobel at once, perfectly sure he knew exactly where she'd said. Then, in an effort to distract him, she added, 'I can't tell you how grateful I am for what you've done to the cottage. I've never had a house to myself before.'

His expression softened. 'I'm sure your parents will miss you terribly. It's a long way from Newcastle to Polgarron. But then, their loss is our gain.'

'My parents are dead,' said Isobel automatically. 'My mother died just a few months ago.'

'I'm sorry.' She hadn't realised it before but in his eyes that provided her with a legitimate reason for wanting to make a new start. 'I wasn't attempting to pry.'

He was, but Isobel chose not to pursue it. 'That's all right,' she said, forcing a smile. 'It's natural that you'd want to know something about your new tenant.'

'Only if you want to tell me,' insisted Luke, evidently prepared to be generous now, and Isobel explained that she was a secondary school teacher, and that she was hoping to find a position in or near Polgarth.

'Well, I'm not absolutely sure of the situation at present,' he said. 'But I have connections with the local education authority, and I'd be happy to make enquiries on your behalf.'

'Thank you.' Isobel would have preferred not to have to feel beholden to him for anything else, but she was aware that a personal endorsement could improve her chances of being offered a position, and she couldn't afford to be churlish.

'Good. Good.' His smile was friendly now, and she hoped she'd passed whatever test he'd felt was warranted. 'Well...' He gestured with the rent book. 'If you hadn't been here, I was just going to push this through the letterbox, but I'm glad we've had this opportunity to cement our association.'

'Yes. So'm I.'

Isobel nodded, but when she stepped aside, in expectation of him going to the door, he sauntered through to the kitchen instead.

Trying not to resent his presumption, Isobel followed him. Things were probably done differently in the country, she told herself, remembering the indifference with which her previous landlord had treated his tenants. She'd never seen Harry Lofthouse unless there'd been some kind of problem with either the plumbing or the heating, the rent having been collected by a monthly direct debit from her account.

Luke was examining the new appliances, but at least he didn't open the fridge door to see what was inside. His interest seemed to stem from a genuine desire to check on the improvements, and Isobel could hardly fault him for that.

'And you expect to move in—when?' he asked, turning to rest against the new Formica-topped counter.

'In a couple of days, I hope,' she answered, half wishing she could offer him a cup of tea. She would have preferred to put their relationship on a more formal footing, but unfortunately she hadn't yet brought the box containing her least mis-matched china from the inn. 'The furniture's being delivered tomorrow.'

'From Newcastle?' He inclined his head. 'You will let me know if you need any assistance, won't you?'

'I'm sure that won't be necessary.' Isobel was grateful to him, but she was beginning to wish that he would go. 'You've done enough.'

'Not nearly.' To her relief he straightened then, and when she retreated to the living room he followed her. 'Perhaps you'd permit me to buy you dinner one evening, as a kind of celebration, perhaps? After you've moved in, of course.'

Isobel's jaw dropped, but she quickly rescued it. 'Oh— I—that's very kind of you, but—'

'But, what?'

'Well, it's not necessary...'

'I know that.' He sounded impatient now. 'But it would

give me a great deal of pleasure.' He paused. 'If you'll agree?'

Isobel shook her head. 'Well...'

'Good.' He took her hesitation as an acceptance. 'I'll be in touch as soon as the phone's connected.'

'The phone?' Isobel's eyes widened. She'd been thinking she would have to get herself a mobile.

'Of course.' Luke looked a little smug now. 'We can't have you living here all alone without one. I've been in touch with the phone company and they're coming to install it at the end of the week. With your approval, of course.'

Isobel was disarmed by his kindness. 'I don't know what to say.'

'It's my pleasure,' he assured her, and this time he made an unsolicited move towards the door. He tapped the rent book against his thigh as he reached for the handle. 'I'll make sure this is amended, too. We can't have a prospective employer addressing you as Miss Dawson, can we?'

It wasn't until after he'd gone that Isobel's doubts about getting socially involved with her landlord resurfaced. She wasn't interested in getting involved with anyone, and although she assured herself that he would probably forget all about his invitation, she didn't want to create any difficulties for herself now that she'd found herself a home.

Still, there was no point in worrying about it now, she conceded, resuming the unpacking she'd been doing before Luke Herrington arrived. And one date didn't constitute an involvement, anyway. If he did insist on taking her to dinner, she would have to explain about the baby and hope it wouldn't make any difference to her lease.

She phoned Michelle from the inn the night before she was due to move into the cottage. Her furniture had arrived, as arranged, that morning, and for a few extra pounds the delivery men had unrolled the carpets in the living room and bedroom, and helped her assemble her bed before they left.

The carpets were not a perfect fit, naturally, but she intended to make some adjustments later. She didn't even have a carpet for the hall and stairs, and she intended to make that her first priority when she went into Polgarth again. For the moment, however, she was content to have a place she could call her own again, and once she'd got the furniture arranged to her satisfaction she'd begin to feel it was a home.

Michelle was delighted to hear that things were going according to plan, and she was particularly pleased when Isobel told her about the phone. 'I must confess, I was a bit anxious about you living there without any form of communication with the outside world,' she said. 'Don't forget to let me have the number as soon as you have it.'

'I won't.' Isobel forced a light tone, but she was beginning to wonder if ringing Michelle had been such a good idea, after all. She sounded so far away, and she was, which automatically led to the thought that other people were a long way away, too. And, unable to help herself, she added, 'How's—everything?'

'Do you mean everything—or everybody?' asked Michelle drily, and Isobel immediately knew that her friend had heard from Jared.

'Whatever,' she said, fighting back the urge to ask the question she was dying to ask. 'Um—have you spoken to Marion?'

'Marion?' Michelle's surprise was not feigned. 'No, I haven't. Should I have?'

'Well, I thought she might have wondered where I was,' muttered Isobel, feeling an absurd desire to burst into tears. 'Does she know I'm not coming back?'

'She does now.'

Michelle's answer was confusing, and Isobel wondered

if she'd misunderstood her before. 'But—I thought you said you hadn't spoken to her.'

'I haven't.' Michelle sighed. 'But Kendall has.'

'Jared!' Even saying his name caused a wave of warmth to invade her stomach. 'You've seen Jared, then?'

'I didn't say that.'

'Then, what—?'

'Oh, Issy, are you sure you want to hear this? I mean, I thought you went away because you wanted to sever the ties between you and Jared. What on earth was the point of that if you're going to ask me about him every time I come on the phone?'

Isobel sniffed. 'I didn't ask you about him.'

'Didn't you?'

Isobel sighed. 'All right. Maybe indirectly.'

'Indirectly, my eye.' Michelle snorted. 'All right. I'll tell you. He rang me last week.'

'Last week!' Isobel had to bite back the urge to ask Michelle why she hadn't bothered to let her know before this. Only the fear of inviting another rebuke kept her silent. 'I—what did he want?'

'What do you think he wanted?' Michelle demanded shortly. 'Needless to say, he didn't get any joy from me.'

'Oh.' Isobel despised herself for the sinking feeling that enveloped her. 'Well, good.'

'Do you mean that?'

Isobel struggled to hide her misery. 'Of course I mean it,' she said, with admirable fortitude. She hesitated. 'I just don't understand how—how he could approach Marion.'

'What you mean is, what has he said to Marion, don't you?' Michelle was cynical. 'Well, from what I gathered, she told him about the letters.'

Isobel caught her breath. 'Marion told Jared about the letters! I don't believe it.'

'Well, I didn't tell him,' said Michelle huffily. 'And he knows all about them.' She gave a sardonic grunt. 'If you ask me, Marion was so shocked when he told her you'd disappeared, she automatically assumed you'd told him about them.'

Isobel licked her dry lips. 'So—did she give him the address that was on the letters?'

'No.' Michelle was positive. 'That was why he rang me. He assumed—quite rightly, as it happens—that I'd know where you were.'

'Oh, Michelle!'

'You didn't want me to give him your address, did you?'

'No!' Isobel was horrified that her friend should even think she might.

'Are you sure?'

'Of course I'm sure.' Isobel made a sound of indignation. 'All right. I admit I was curious about how—how he was taking it. My leaving, I mean. But it was the right thing to do.' She paused. 'Wasn't it?'

Michelle didn't answer for a moment. Then, almost wearily, she conceded, 'I guess.'

'You guess?' Isobel felt anxiety pricking her nerves.

'Hey…' Michelle groaned. 'I don't profess to be an expert on human relationships. Sure, your affair with Kendall was going nowhere. And, in your present condition, I'd say that going away has probably saved you a hell of a lot of heartache, not to mention making it easier for—well, for everyone, if you get my meaning. But— oh.' She expelled a weary breath. 'I have to admit to feeling a bit sorry for him. Kendall, that is. I guess I thought that he'd feel really peeved when he found you'd walked out on him and all, but that deep down he'd be relieved. Hell, Elizabeth's father is Goldman-Lewis, after all.' She paused. 'Jared must know he took a hell of a risk in contacting your sister. Particularly as we all know how desperate she is to cosy up to the Goldmans.'

Isobel's throat was dry. 'So what are you saying?'

'I don't know.' Michelle sighed. 'I don't know what I'm saying. Whatever it is, I'm pretty sure you're better off out of it.'

Isobel blew out a breath. 'So—did he say anything else?'

'What about?'

'The letters, I suppose.' Isobel wished she could see her friend's face. 'Was he—worried? Angry? What?'

'I'd say he was—hurt,' admitted Michelle, turning the knife. 'I'm sorry, Issy. But you did ask.'

'I know.'

'As far as the letters were concerned, he asked me if I'd known about them. I said yes. I saw no point in lying about that.'

'No.' Isobel pressed two fingers to her throbbing temple. 'I suppose I should have told him.'

'What? And have him turn up on your doorstep within days of your leaving? Oh, yeah, Issy. That would have been the sensible thing to do.'

Isobel shook her head. 'Well...' She tried to be optimistic. 'It looks as if I've done it, doesn't it? Made a complete break. Just what I wanted.'

'Why don't I find that as convincing as I should?' asked Michelle sardonically. 'But, okay. Enough about Jared Kendall. How are you? Have you registered with a doctor yet?'

'No, but I will, once I'm settled into the cottage,' Isobel promised. 'And I'll ring you just as soon as the phone's been installed.'

There didn't seem much more to say right then, but after she'd rung off Isobel wondered why she hadn't told her friend about Luke Herrington's invitation. Was it really because she hadn't considered it important enough to mention? Or would it be truer to say that so long as Michelle didn't know about it, she couldn't tell Jared?

*   *   *

Isobel spent the first day at the cottage trying to get her bedroom in some kind of order. The downstairs rooms could wait, but she was still plagued by feelings of nausea, and it was important that she had somewhere where she could rest and relax. Besides, she got tired quickly these days, and she had no desire to have to tackle her bed at a time when she wanted nothing so much as to fall into it.

The paper in the bedroom was light and airy, sprigs of mauve blossom on a white background that added space to what was really quite a small room. It might not have been her choice of decoration, but she quite liked it, and with her own rose-printed curtains billowing at the open windows, it looked very pretty.

The windows themselves were set under the eaves, the ceiling sloping slightly at that side of the room. She managed to position her bed so that she was able to see out of the windows when she awoke in the morning. For the first time in her life, she had an uninterrupted view.

Her clothes were the next things to unpack. She'd been living out of suitcases for the past four weeks and it was going to be so nice to know where everything was again. On top of which, there were cartons containing shoes and other odds and ends that she'd had stored along with the furniture, as well as handbags and winter clothing that she hadn't had an immediate use for.

Before she knew it, it was one o'clock, and after casting a satisfied glance around the room she went downstairs to make herself some lunch. She was making good progress, and she had no intention of overdoing it. It wasn't as if she had a deadline.

Her breath caught in her throat. Deadlines were for people who had something to do and somewhere to go. She didn't. At least, not yet. And it was annoying to realise that even something as innocuous as that could bring back painful memories of her life as it used to be.

It was a short step from that to allowing thoughts of the

conversation she'd had with Michelle the previous evening to fill her mind. She didn't want to think about what her friend had told her, or face the doubts that had been evident in Michelle's voice. It was enough that they'd tormented her sleep without them destroying what little pleasure she'd found in moving into the cottage.

She was making herself a sandwich when a shadow passed the kitchen window. Someone had walked along the side of the house, she realised, and she was hardly surprised when there was a knock at the back door. Luke Herrington again, she thought frustratedly. Dear God, he hadn't wasted any time.

She wondered whether, if she'd still been working upstairs, she'd have risked not answering the door. But, no. Her car was parked in the lane outside, and all the windows were open.

She glanced down at the cropped vest she was wearing, together with denim shorts that were frayed and bleached almost white in places from frequent washings, and pulled a face. She'd changed before tackling the unpacking, guessing, quite rightly as it turned out, that she'd find it hot work, but now she wished she wasn't wearing something quite so revealing. Not that anyone who didn't know would guess that the waistband of the shorts was abnormally tight. And, taking a deep breath, she opened the door—to Jared.

CHAPTER EIGHT

DIZZINESS assailed her, and she clung to the handle of the door, praying she wasn't about to faint. Isobel had never fainted before, and if she did so now Jared might easily suspect that there was something wrong with her. And she couldn't have that.

All the same, as she stood there, struggling to recover her senses, she couldn't deny how good it was to see him again. Her eyes moved with indecent haste over his lean tanned face—surely paler than she remembered, his eyes narrowed and guarded behind his glasses—to the muscled strength of his arms, exposed below the short sleeves of a black tee shirt. Pleated khaki trousers completed his outfit, a matching jacket hooked carelessly over one shoulder.

How had he found her? she wondered, as the dizziness subsided. Michelle had insisted that she hadn't told him anything and surely Marion never would...

'Surprise, surprise,' he said at last, when it appeared that she was incapable of making the first overture. 'If it isn't the incredible disappearing woman!'

Isobel stiffened. 'Don't be sarcastic.'

'Why not?' He shifted his weight from one foot to the other. 'Believe me, sarcastic is good.'

'As opposed to what?' Isobel tried desperately to sound as if he hadn't just swept the ground out from under her, but it was obvious that Jared wasn't in the mood to humour her.

'Take it from me, you don't want to go there,' he remarked, his voice clipped and unfriendly. 'May I come in?'

Isobel gave a shrug and moved aside, holding onto the

door as he stepped into the small kitchen. As he'd gone to the trouble of seeking her out, he deserved an explanation—albeit an edited one. She just wished she knew what she was going to say.

'I was just making myself a sandwich,' she murmured rather obviously after closing the door. 'Would you like one?'

Jared swung his jacket off his shoulder and folded it over one arm. 'No, thanks,' he said, and she realised he wasn't just unfriendly, he was hostile. 'I just want to know why you didn't tell me you were leaving.'

Isobel swallowed a little convulsively and moved back to the counter. Picking up the knife again, she started buttering a slice of bread, only to utter an involuntary cry of protest when he snatched the knife out of her hand and tossed it into the sink.

'Dammit, answer me!'

Isobel quivered, her hand going automatically to protect her stomach. 'Are you mad?' she exclaimed tremulously. 'What gives you the right to think you can come here and intimidate me?'

Jared stared at her, breathing hard, and for a second she thought he meant to do her some actual physical harm. But then, uttering a harsh obscenity, he turned away.

'God knows,' he said, at last, when he'd got himself under control again. 'It's obvious you don't give a damn about what I think.'

Isobel expelled the breath she'd hardly been aware she was holding. 'I—I suppose it does look that way,' she muttered awkwardly, wringing her hands before pushing them into the back pockets of her shorts.

Jared turned his head to give her a pitying glance. 'How's that for understatement?' he asked contemptuously. 'God, I've had some pretty foul things done to me in my time, but this beats all!'

'I'm sorry—'

'I bet you are. That I've found you, I guess.' He grimaced. 'Who'd have thought I'd have to thank your sister for anything?'

Isobel stared at him. 'Marion told you where I was?'

'Oh, yeah.' He was sardonic. 'And gave me written instructions on how to get here! Yeah, right.'

Isobel blinked. 'Then, how——?'

'How did I find you?' He turned back to face her, swiping away the sweat that had beaded on his forehead and dampened the hair at his temples. 'Give me one good reason why I should tell you that.'

'I can't.' Isobel shook her head, and then, because she could see he was exhausted, she gestured towards the front room. 'Look—why don't you go and sit down? Surely you'll have a beer or something? It is lunchtime.'

'Is it?' He sounded weary. 'I don't even know what day it is any more.'

Isobel sighed. 'It's Thursday,' she said, waiting for him to do as she'd asked. 'Have you had anything to eat or drink today?'

'Don't tell me you care,' he taunted bitterly, and, refusing to answer him, she reached for a clean knife out of the drawer.

She didn't move when he eventually gave in and walked past her, even though the heated brush of his arm against her back caused every nerve in her body to rise up in protest. Instead, she forced herself to finish making her sandwich, and then made another, just in case. She'd already made the tea, and, after adding another cup and saucer and a bottle of beer to the tray, she took a deep breath and carried it into the other room.

He'd tossed his jacket onto the back of a chair and was presently standing staring out of the window. Now that the windows were clean, they gleamed brilliantly between leaded lights, showing up the tangled wilderness of the garden outside.

'I've made you a sandwich,' she said, setting the tray on the coffee table and perching on the edge of the sofa closest to it. 'It's only egg and tomato, I'm afraid.'

He turned. 'Egg and *tomato*?' he echoed. 'I thought you didn't like uncooked tomatoes.'

'Oh—' Isobel could feel herself colouring. 'Well, I don't, usually. But this tastes all right.' She could hardly admit to having a sudden craving for the fruit. 'And they're yellow tomatoes anyway.'

Jared arched a disbelieving brow. 'Are you sure it's not just another attempt to prove to me that you've changed?' he asked flatly. He walked towards her. 'Is this for me?'

He'd picked up the bottle of beer, and she nodded shakily, aware that for another anxious moment she'd been half afraid he was going to touch her. But he didn't. As she buried her teeth in one of the quartered sandwiches she'd cut for herself, praying that by getting something substantial inside her she could quell the uneasy turbulence of her stomach, Jared twisted off the cap and retired to the window again.

He propped his hips on the narrow ledge and raised the bottle to his lips, and she had to steel herself not to watch the muscles in his throat moving beneath the tanned skin. It was hard enough trying to ignore him watching her as she struggled to get the sandwich down, without torturing herself with the knowledge that what she really wanted him to do was take her to bed.

Which was madness...

'Have you spoken to your father yet?'

His question caught her by surprise, and she almost choked on a crust, staring at him with watering eyes. 'My father?'

'Don't look as if you don't know what I'm talking about.' Jared's tone was biting. 'That is what you're doing here, isn't it? Setting up house on his doorstep, hoping he's had a change of heart.'

Isobel gasped. 'What do you know about my father?'

'About as much as you do, by the sound of it,' he retorted contemptuously. And then, as if regretting his cruel words, 'Marion said you'd found some letters.'

Isobel quivered, getting to her feet and rubbing nervous palms over the seat of her shorts. 'She had no right to tell you anything.'

'I'm sure she would agree with you,' Jared concurred, giving her a bitter look. 'You certainly believe in covering your tracks, don't you?'

'Do you blame me?'

Her response was automatic, and she determinedly crushed the emotion she felt when she saw the spasm of pain that crossed his face.

'I guess not,' he said at last, flatly, weighing the empty bottle in his hands. 'If this is what you really want.'

'It is.'

'Are you sure?' He stared at her disbelievingly. 'My God, Belle, if you really don't want to see me again, then I'm going to have to live with it. But was there any need to put the length of the country between us?'

'I think so.'

'Why? *Why?*' he demanded, almost dropping the bottle in his agitation and then bending to place it on the floor at his feet with hands that were obviously unsteady. 'Do you really hate me that much?'

She didn't hate him at all; that was the trouble. And Isobel's heart ached at the obvious confusion in his expression. 'You shouldn't have come after me,' she said, staring down at the toes of her scuffed trainers. 'You must have known—'

'What?' He waited for her to go on, but she couldn't. 'What should I have known? That having sex with me in your mother's kitchen was your way of finishing it? Of showing me how little it meant to you?'

'That's not true.' She couldn't let him think that. 'I told you at the time…'

'Oh, yeah, you told me,' he muttered. 'What was it you said: *Just do it*? I guess I should have known then that you were planning on walking out on me.'

Isobel's sigh was shaky. 'It just seemed—'

'Easier that way?'

'Something like that.' Isobel tucked her thumbs into her waistband.

'So—' Jared got up from the windowsill. 'Have you seen him?'

'Seen who?' For a moment Isobel's mind was a total blank.

'Your father, of course,' said Jared tiredly. 'I wish you'd told me about those letters.'

'I only found them that afternoon—' Isobel broke off, not wanting to bring up the events of that afternoon again, but he had always had the uncanny ability to read her thoughts.

'*That* afternoon?' he echoed. 'Do you mean when you were crawling around the loft at Jesmond Dene?'

Isobel nodded. 'Yes.'

'The case,' he said suddenly, and she knew he was remembering what she had said about it. 'They were in that case, weren't they?' His eyes narrowed. 'Was that when you decided to give me the push?'

'No!' She was vehement. 'They had nothing to do with it.' She took a calming breath. 'What did Marion tell you?'

Jared's lips curled. 'Not a lot.'

'But enough to find me.'

'Hardly.' He paused. 'If I hadn't let her think I knew about the letters, she'd never have let the name slip.'

'The name of the village?'

'I wish.' Jared was cynical. 'No, not the name of the village. Just Tregarth or Tregarron; she wasn't sure which. And the fact that it was in Cornwall.'

'Tregarron?' Isobel frowned in confusion.

'As I said, she was only groping for the address the letters had come from at the time.'

'But how did you find it? Tregarth isn't even the name of the place.'

'Tell me about it.' Jared grimaced. 'That was when I had the bright idea of trying your friend, Michelle. But, as you probably know, I don't rate very highly in her opinion either.'

He looked as if he would have liked to have left it there, but she was obviously waiting for him to go on, so after a few moments he said, 'Then I tried looking up the names in a road atlas. But the only listings there were in Wales, and Marion had definitely said Cornwall.'

'So what did you do?' Isobel was amazed at his persistence. 'How on earth did you expect to find me even with the name of the town?'

'A town I might have had difficulty with,' he agreed wryly. 'But I went on the assumption that, as I hadn't heard of them, they were probably villages; hamlets, something like that. A strange woman moving into a small village would surely arouse some curiosity. At least, that's what I was banking on, anyway.'

Isobel shook her head. 'But I might not have moved into the village.'

'I know that.' Jared shrugged wearily. 'I'm not denying it was a gamble. But when you're desperate enough, you'll go to any lengths to make it work.'

Isobel hesitated. 'Yet you said the names weren't listed.'

'They weren't.' Jared nodded. 'So I ran them though the computer instead. It's amazing what you can find out if you're determined to get a result.'

'And?'

'And—I found the name of a house: Tregarth Hall, Polgarron. As there weren't any Tregarron houses or halls in the program I was using, I decided to run with it. I figured Marion was unlikely to have remembered the name unless it was a particular place.'

Isobel was reluctantly impressed. 'Even so...' she murmured.

'Hell, I know. I could have been making entirely the wrong connection. But, obviously, I wasn't.'

Isobel was shaking her head, staggered at the success he'd had, when another thought struck her. Her mouth went dry. 'You—you didn't go to Tregarth Hall, did you?' she faltered. 'Oh, God, as far as I know, they don't even know I'm here.'

Jared gave her a scornful look. 'Oh, yeah,' he said. 'I was going to do that, wasn't I? I didn't even know if this was the right village, let alone the right house. What do you think I'd have said, hmm?' He pretended to think for a minute. 'Oh—I've got it: *Hey, I'm looking for a woman who thinks you gave her up for adoption—what? Twenty-six years ago? Got any idea where she is?*'

Isobel held up her head. 'That's not funny.'

'You're telling me.' Jared was bitter. 'Believe it or not, I recognised the car. I was driving around the village, trying to concoct a convincing story to tell the publican at the Black Bull, and there it was. Parked at the gate.' His lips twisted. 'So you haven't contacted this man yet? But you intend to.'

'I don't know.' Isobel didn't want to admit it, but she was having some doubts now that she was here. 'I'm not sure if it's the right thing to do.'

'I'm bloody sure it's not,' said Jared forcefully. 'For God's sake, Belle, you don't know anything about the man. He could be a serial child molester for all you know.'

'Oh, thanks.' Isobel caught her breath. 'It's good to know you think I might come from such distinguished stock!'

'Don't be so—stupid!' Jared bit off the epithet he had been going to use and grasped her shoulders. With his fingers digging into her flesh, he thrust his face close to hers. 'I don't give a damn who he is. As far as I'm concerned, he's not important. You are. All I'm trying to say is that if he'd been any kind of a father, he wouldn't have abandoned your mother when she needed him all those years ago.'

Isobel was trembling, as much from the goosebumps his touch was causing as from the violence of his reaction. 'He—he's my uncle,' she got out jerkily, and used his momentary lack of concentration to free herself from his hands. 'He's my father's brother.'

Jared dragged his spectacles from his nose and blinked myopically at her. 'My God!'

'It's true.' Isobel realised she had to elaborate and went on, 'I was the result of a brief liaison he'd had when he was in London visiting his solicitor. That's where I was born. He didn't know anything about me until my mother was killed and the authorities discovered his name on my birth certificate.'

Jared replaced his glasses. 'So how come you ended up with your real uncle? Didn't anyone think to tell you the truth?'

'Not until I read the letters, no,' admitted Isobel uncomfortably. 'It's a long story. I'm sure you're not really interested.'

Jared arched a speculative brow. 'Wait a minute: you said you'd never met him.'

'I haven't.'

'Your own uncle?' Jared made a disbelieving sound. 'How the hell did they manage that?'

'It sounds incredible, I know.' Isobel heaved a sigh. 'But I didn't know my father—my adoptive father, that is—had any brothers or sisters. It's true. I wouldn't lie about something like that.'

Jared was obviously finding it difficult to get a handle on what she was saying, and, deciding she had nothing to lose, Isobel quickly outlined the conditions George Dorland had made at the time of her adoption. 'There was obviously no love lost between them,' she murmured unwillingly. 'As far as I know, there's been no contact since then.'

'But why couldn't your real father take care of you?' exclaimed Jared, and once again Isobel was obliged to explain the circumstances behind Robert Dorland's appeal to her mother.

'Dear God,' Jared said at last, and, glimpsing the look of repugnance that had darkened his face as he'd absorbed what she was saying, Isobel wondered if what he'd learned had somehow cheapened her in his eyes.

'Things were different then,' she said hurriedly, aware that she was trying to excuse what had happened. 'And— and if his wife—my aunt—couldn't have children, it would have been quite a blow to her.'

'Not to mention exposing his behaviour,' remarked Jared scornfully, and Isobel caught her breath.

'You know what they say about people in glass houses,' she observed curtly, and had the satisfaction of seeing the heat darken his tanned face.

'I hope you're not comparing our relationship to a one-night stand with some—some—'

'Hooker?' supplied Isobel coldly, and once again Jared's colour deepened at the accusation.

'I was going to say with some woman he'd met by accident,' he retorted harshly. 'Dammit, Belle, you said yourself their association had been brief. Stop trying to put words into my mouth. You know our relationship isn't like that.'

'Do I?'

He didn't bother to dignify that with an answer. 'I just don't know how he could have done such a thing,' he muttered, his mind on other things.

'Done what?' she asked. 'Gone in for one-night stands

or abandoned me? I guess you'd say he can't be a very honourable man.'

'I was talking about George Dorland, actually,' said Jared shortly. 'I was wondering how the hell he could cut his own brother out of his life.'

Isobel sighed now. 'He must have thought it was for the best.'

'For whom?' Jared was sceptical. 'I still don't see why he kept the truth from you.'

'Because he probably guessed—rightly, as it happens— that I'd be curious about him,' said Isobel ruefully. 'Look, do you mind if we talk about something else? I've told you as much as I know about it. And I still haven't decided whether I'm going to tell him who I am or not.'

'Haven't you?'

Jared's tone was gentler now, and Isobel despised herself for the weakening she felt towards him. If he didn't go soon she was in danger of saying something really stupid, and she couldn't afford to make any more mistakes.

'No,' she said now. Then, with deliberate emphasis, 'How's Elizabeth?'

The look that crossed his face then was chilling. If her earlier words hadn't struck a nerve, it was obvious that that question had. 'I guess that's a polite way of saying I've wasted my time in coming here,' he said darkly. His mouth curled. 'Since when did my association with my wife have anything to do with us?'

CHAPTER NINE

THE engineer from the telephone company arrived the next morning before Isobel had had time to swallow the dry toast she usually ate at breakfast. She was still nauseous some mornings and she thought the man looked at her a little oddly when she let him in.

She knew she was pale and she guessed her lack of colour had drawn his attention to the hollow circles around her eyes. But there was nothing she could do about it now. Her first night at the cottage hadn't been as restful as she'd anticipated, and it wasn't just the trauma of Jared's visit that had left her feeling so tired and depressed.

The unfamiliar quiet of the village had unsettled her, and the creaks and groans as the boards in the cottage contracted had kept her constantly on edge. Perhaps she should get herself a dog, she'd speculated, dragging herself out of bed at eight o'clock, and, confronting her haggard reflection in the mirror, she was glad Jared couldn't see her now.

By the time she'd quelled a rising surge of nausea, cleaned her teeth and pulled on a baggy tee shirt and sweat pants, the engineer was on her doorstep. Happily he wasn't a young man, so she didn't feel so bad about looking a mess. All the same, she wished the cottage had a shower. She missed washing her hair every day.

After telling the man where she'd like the phone situated, Isobel went into the kitchen and made some tea. Then, after swallowing a slice of toast, she felt well enough to offer him some refreshment, smiling rather wanly when he asked if she was feeling all right.

'I think I must have a cold coming on,' she offered, not

wanting to tell him what was really wrong with her. 'It's a lovely morning, isn't it?'

'Not bad,' the man agreed, thanking her for his tea. He glanced around, noticing the unpacked boxes. 'I guess you've just moved in.'

'Yesterday,' she acknowledged, feeling a pang at the memory of Jared's departure. 'Do—do you live in the village yourself?'

'No. I live in Polgarth,' he answered, putting the cup down and resuming his task, but although Isobel was sure he'd have been willing to go on talking, she made an excuse and retreated to the kitchen again.

It didn't take him long to install the phone. Apparently there'd been a line to the cottage when it was last occupied, and it was just a matter of reconnecting the wires. Isobel had her hands in a bowl of soapy water, and was staring unseeingly though the kitchen window, when the engineer came to tell her he was finished, and she hurriedly dried her hands before taking the clipboard he offered to her.

'If you'll just sign here,' he said, indicating the job sheet, and Isobel signed her name and accompanied him to the door.

'Your name's Dorland?' The man had glanced at the sheet and now he halted in the open doorway. 'I suppose you're related to the Dorlands at Tregarth Hall?'

Isobel swallowed. 'I—no,' she said, aware that a trace of colour had entered her cheeks at the lie. 'Are there other Dorlands in the village?'

'Just the family at Tregarth.' The man nodded. 'There've been Dorlands there for—well, for as long as I can remember anyway.'

Isobel hesitated. 'You know them?'

'Only slightly.' The man grimaced. 'I've fixed Mrs Dorland's phone a time or two, but I don't know the rest of them very well.' He grinned. 'Well, I'd better be going. I'll never get finished at this rate. Thanks for the tea.'

'Thank you.'

Isobel forced a smile, but after she'd closed the door she leant back against it, feeling utterly bereft. In his letters, Robert Dorland had insisted his wife couldn't have children. So who else was living at the Hall?

Of course, he could have married again, she considered, pushing away from the door and glancing somewhat bleakly about her. That was something she hadn't considered, and she wondered once again if she hadn't made the biggest mistake of her life in coming here. It was only a matter of time before someone told Robert Dorland that there was someone of the same name, with a northern accent, living at Raven Cottage. How long would it take for him to suspect who she might be?

Would he care?

With tears pricking at her eyes, she went to finish the dishes. Perhaps she should have found herself a bolt-hole nearer to the people who really cared about her, instead of risking being rejected for the second time in her life. Jared was right. If Robert Dorland had cared about her, he would never have abandoned her. Whatever conceit had made her think he'd ever want to see her again?

Drying her hands, she went back into the living room again. The newly installed phone was a distraction and she determinedly reached for the receiver. She'd done it now, so there was no point in feeling sorry for herself. It was time to tell her sister where she was.

She phoned Marion's office, and for once she seemed genuinely relieved to hear from her. 'When that Kendall man told me you'd given up your apartment and moved away, I couldn't believe it,' she exclaimed. 'Are you all right?'

'I'm fine. And—and his name is Jared,' said Isobel automatically. 'I—wanted to wait until I knew where I was going to be living before giving you an address.'

'Well, I suppose I can understand that.' Marion was surprisingly amiable. 'I dare say you suspected he might contact me for information as to your whereabouts, and the less I knew, the better.'

'Well—'

'And you were right.' Marion snorted with satisfaction. 'He did come to me, and I sent him away with a flea in his ear.'

'You—saw—Jared?' Isobel's tongue circled her upper lip. He hadn't told her he'd seen Marion.

'No.' Marion clicked her tongue. 'He phoned me. I don't know how he had the nerve to do it. I mean, he knows I'm a friend of his wife's.'

Isobel sank down weakly onto the arm of the nearest chair. 'You're saying you didn't tell him anything, then?' she ventured softly, and Marion sounded almost offended at the suggestion.

'As if I would,' she said. 'Oh, I'm not denying he tried to pump me about those letters. But I told him. I said, It's nothing whatsoever to do with you.' She chuckled smugly. 'He got the message.'

'Did he?'

Isobel felt a momentary twinge of humour. If Marion only knew, she thought wryly. She'd be mortified to think she'd let anything slip. She thought she'd been so clever, when in fact Jared had been more clever than either of them.

'So, come on: where are you?' asked Marion impatiently. 'I think it's a good idea, by the way. Making a complete break like this. It was obvious that the man was never going to leave you alone so long as you stayed in Newcastle. I suppose Michelle Chambers knew all about it. You and she taking a holiday indeed! I should have suspected that her husband wouldn't have been very enthusiastic if he'd thought you were trying to split them up.'

'It was nothing like that,' said Isobel, a little crossly. Marion always had the knack of rubbing her up the wrong way. 'Michelle just—helped me move my things. Their estate car holds so much more than my Fiesta.'

'I see.' Marion absorbed this without comment. 'So you'd obviously been thinking about it for some time.'

'Well, it was time for a change,' agreed Isobel, not wanting to go too deeply into her reasons for leaving. 'With Mum dying and all, it seemed like a good time to make a fresh start.'

'And I suppose those letters you found couldn't have helped,' said Marion thoughtfully. 'I can't imagine why Mum kept them. I'm sure Daddy knew nothing about it. He'd have felt—offended, I think, if he had.'

'I had a right to know,' insisted Isobel, not prepared to compromise on that principle. 'He had no right to keep it from me. Not once I was old enough to understand.'

'To understand what?' Marion was scathing. 'Isobel, he knew what a sentimental—emotional—creature you are. I expect he doubted your ability to view what he'd done in a sane and rational way.'

'Well, I suppose he was right about that.' Isobel drew a breath. 'I do find it hard to believe how he could just cut his own brother out of his life.'

'Well, you would.' Marion sighed, and then, apparently deciding it wasn't worth arguing about, she turned back to the reason why Isobel had called. 'So, where are you? You don't know how hard it's been to convince Emily that her auntie Isobel hasn't gone to heaven, like her nana.'

'Oh, I'm sorry.' Isobel felt genuinely concerned for her niece. 'I never thought she'd think that.'

'I could say you don't think, period,' remarked Marion drily. 'But never mind that; give me your address.'

Isobel moistened her lips. 'It's—Raven Cottage,' she said reluctantly. 'Polgarron.'

'Polgarron!' Marion's gasp was audible. 'You're staying with Uncle Robert?'

Uncle Robert!

Isobel was surprised at the way his name tripped off her sister's tongue. She had yet to come to terms with the fact that he'd been her father's brother, let alone...

'As if,' she said now. 'The Dorlands live at Tregarth Hall.' And, recalling what Jared had told her, 'You remember the address, don't you?'

'Oh—yes.' Marion still sounded agitated. 'So, have you been in touch with him?'

'Not yet.'

'But you're thinking of it, aren't you?' Marion gave an impatient exclamation. 'Of course you are. Why else would you have moved to Polgarth when you had the whole country to choose from? Oh, Isobel, I can't believe you'd do such a thing!'

Isobel was taken aback at the vehemence of Marion's condemnation. 'Why not?'

'Why not?' Marion spoke fiercely. 'You know how Daddy felt about him, about what he'd done. If it hadn't been for my mother, he'd never have agreed to the arrangement.'

'Yes, I had gathered that.' But Isobel was surprised that Marion had garnered as much from the brief glance she'd taken of the letter Isobel had shown her.

'There you are, then. Surely it's obvious that neither of the parents wanted you to know about it—about him.'

'Then why keep the letters?'

'How should I know?' Marion was irritable now. 'You know what Mum was like. She hated to throw anything away.'

'Even so...'

'Even so, what? You're not suggesting she left them

there deliberately for you to find? Come on, Isobel, she couldn't be sure you would be the one to find them. Malcolm or I could have volunteered to clear out the loft.'

'Could have' being the operative words, thought Isobel cynically. Her mother would have had a fairly good idea that she'd get the job.

'Anyway, I still haven't decided what I'm going to do,' she admitted. 'For the present, I'm just going to play it by ear.'

'Well, you'd better give me your phone number,' said Marion shortly. 'Fortunately, we haven't found a buyer for the house yet. I'd hate to think what I'd have done if I'd needed to get in touch with you urgently.'

'In an emergency, Michelle would have given you my address,' said Isobel practically, beginning to feel the familiar sense of oppression Marion's domineering attitude always evoked. She gave her sister the number, and then declared with forced brightness, 'I'd better go now. I've got a lot to do today and this call must be costing me the earth.'

'But you'll keep me informed of what you're doing, won't you?' Marion persisted, and Isobel knew exactly what she meant. 'And you will think seriously before doing anything—rash. I mean, Mum and Daddy didn't have to adopt you, you know. The least you can do is respect their wishes now they're dead.'

Isobel made some non-committal response, but after she'd hung up the phone she found herself wondering if Marion didn't have a point. Yet the letters had been there for her to find, and surely someone who'd wanted so desperately to keep the facts of her adoption hidden would have burned them long ago.

She scrambled some eggs for her lunch and then, realising it was time she familiarised herself with her surroundings, she decided to go for a walk. She needed some bread, and she knew that she couldn't remain a prisoner in her own home for ever. She didn't want to admit that she had wondered if Jared would come back, and the prospect of spending the afternoon listening for the familiar sound of his car in the lane outside was too pitiful to countenance. He'd gone; she had to accept it and get on with her life.

The village consisted of little more than a main street with two pubs, a church and its attendant vicarage, and the general stores-cum-post office taking up most of one side. There were several substantial houses, standing in their own grounds, with poplar and cypress trees set behind wrought-iron fences, and a row of what might once have been miners' cottages that had been lovingly restored and maintained. An open expanse marked the village green, with a small pond where a family of ducks clucked in lazy contentment. The gardens she could see were still bright with flowering shrubs, and, noticing the late-flowering lilies and richly coloured dahlias, Isobel was unhappily reminded of the unkempt gardens at the cottage. She would have to tackle them soon, and she wondered if there was a lawn mower lurking in the garden shed.

There were few people about. She saw an elderly man walking his dog and some young children careering up and down on bicycles. A group of teenagers were perched on the wall outside the village stores, and she was conscious of them watching her as she walked towards them. But she was used to teenagers, and they soon lost interest when she didn't react to their subtle intimidation.

Entering the stores was far more daunting. Although she kept telling herself that she had as much right to be here as anyone else, she couldn't help the quiver of apprehension she felt when the two women who had been chatting with the postmistress broke off what they were saying when she came in. She was aware that they all watched her take a loaf of bread from the display and approach the till, and despite herself her hands trembled as she fumbled her purse from her bag.

But before she could offer payment, a curious tremor swept over her. It was not like any feeling she'd ever had before, and for an awful moment she wondered if she was going to faint. She took a trembling breath as the sensation that she could only liken to butterflies in her stomach caused her to grope urgently for the edge of the counter, and, as if her weakness had breached their standoffishness, all three women hurried to her aid.

'Here, sit you down,' said the younger of the two women who had been chatting to the shopkeeper. She dragged an old cane chair that had been standing in a corner forward and helped Isobel into it as the postmistress hurried away to get her a glass of water. 'There, just take it easy.'

'You've been overdoing it.' The other woman was not to be outdone. 'We all know what it's like when you've just moved house. And it's been so hot.'

Isobel managed a faint smile. Evidently they all knew who she was. But her hand went automatically to the curve of her abdomen and she prayed that this wasn't a forerunner to her losing her baby.

The shopkeeper came back with the water and Isobel sipped it gratefully. But she was aware of them exchanging knowing glances above her head and she guessed that little escaped their notice.

'Feeling better?'

It was the shopkeeper who spoke now. A plump woman, in her late forties, Isobel guessed. She had a friendly smile, and Isobel nodded. 'Much better,' she agreed, looking round at them. 'I don't know what happened. I'm not normally affected by the heat.'

'You have to look after yourself when you're in your condition,' declared the second woman sharply, and Isobel

realised she wasn't the only one to be embarrassed by such
plain speaking.

'Sarah,' protested the shopkeeper, giving her a horrified
look, and the younger woman took the opportunity to in-
troduce herself.

'I'm Joanne James,' she said ruefully. 'And you'll have
to forgive Mrs Creighton. She has a reputation to uphold.'

'I can speak for myself, thank you.' Sarah Creighton
regarded the other women indignantly. 'And it's not as if
we didn't all guess what was wrong with Mrs—Ms—'

'Dorland,' Isobel conceded reluctantly. 'And it's all
right. It's not as if I'll be able to hide it for long.'

'Dorland,' echoed Joanne, arching an inquisitive brow,
but to Isobel's relief the woman who owned the shop came
unwittingly to her rescue.

'And isn't that just like a man?' she remarked slyly,
taking the empty glass from Isobel's hand. 'Never around
when you need them.'

Isobel forced herself to get up from the chair. 'I'm—
separated from my partner,' she said, wincing at yet another lie. 'And—well, I think I'm all right now.' She found
her purse again. 'If I can just pay for the bread...'

Yet, despite her eagerness to get away from the women,
Isobel left the shop with some reluctance. She should have
brought the car, she thought worriedly, facing the walk
home with real trepidation. Perhaps she had been overdoing things. There was no doubt that she had been bending and lifting for the better part of the last two days.

She made it back to the cottage without further incident
and let herself into her own domain with an enormous
feeling of relief. It was unfortunate, perhaps, that the facts
of her situation were likely to be common knowledge
around the village very shortly, but at least she'd broken
the ice. And cut off any speculation as to the possible
whereabouts of her 'partner', she acknowledged wryly. Or,

at least, she hoped she had. So long as no one had seen Jared's car and jumped to the wrong conclusion.

Jared...

A sob rose unbidden into her throat and she fought it back. Damn, was she never going to be able to think about him without feeling close to tears? Jared was history; he had to be. That was the reason she was here, for heaven's sake. The idea of contacting Robert Dorland had come much later.

And was likely to remain dormant, she thought, somewhat painfully. After what the telephone engineer had said, she was having serious doubts about Robert Dorland's honesty, and the conversation she had had with Marion had only added to her uncertainty. The question of whether he'd have ignored her existence for so long if he'd really cared about her couldn't be ignored. And what if she wasn't his daughter? Her sister's opinion of her biological mother couldn't entirely be dismissed either.

The jangle of the phone almost scared the life out of her. She'd got out of the habit of hearing a phone ring. At the hotel, she'd made calls, but she couldn't remember the last time she'd received one. And it was weeks since she'd had a phone of her own.

But as she went to answer it another quiver rippled across her abdomen and she halted abruptly, pressing an anxious hand to her stomach. And felt it again. A faint, but unmistakable tremor that she suddenly identified. It was the baby, she thought incredulously. She could feel her baby moving.

Her excitement was so intense she wanted to share it with somebody, and she hurried to pick up the receiver, hoping against hope that it might be Michelle. She'd left her new number on Michelle's answering machine that morning and it was about the time her friend got in from school.

'Polgarth 4542,' she said breathily, after snatching up

the phone, and then was taken aback when a man's voice answered.

'Miss Dorland?'

'Yes,' she said wearily, swallowing her disappointment. 'Who is this?'

'Luke Herrington here,' declared her landlord pleasantly. 'Just checking that everything's okay.'

'Oh—yes.' Isobel endeavoured to sound more upbeat than before. 'Everything's fine, thank you.' She managed a short laugh. 'You're my first caller.'

'Ah, you mean the phone,' he responded lightly. 'Yes. I have to admit, I had to pull a few strings there.'

'Did you?' Isobel realised that sounded as if she was questioning his integrity and amended it. 'You did.' She took a breath. 'Well—thanks.'

'It was my pleasure,' he assured her warmly. 'If there's anything I can do to help, you only have to ask.'

'You're very kind.'

'Not at all.' He waited a beat. 'By the way, you haven't forgotten about my invitation, have you?'

Isobel grimaced, glad he couldn't see her expression at that moment. 'Er—your invitation?' she murmured faintly, hoping he would take the hint and make some excuse for not being able to follow up on it. 'I'm afraid I've been too busy to think about anything except how exhausting moving house can be.'

'You've obviously been working too hard,' he said firmly, and she could tell from his tone that had no intention of letting her off the hook. 'What you need is an escape from all your endeavours, however worthy they might be. An evening of pampering, where the only effort that will be expected of you is to make yourself look beautiful. And that will take no effort at all.'

Isobel suppressed a groan. 'Oh, really, I—'

'You're going to turn me down?'

'Would you mind?'

'You've made other arrangements?' His voice was cooler. 'I'm sorry. I thought you said you didn't know anyone in the district.'

'I don't.' Isobel realised she was in danger of arousing his suspicions. 'Um—what time were you thinking of?'

'Well, not early,' he exclaimed, the warmth seeping back into his voice. 'I'm sure you've had a busy day, and you'll need time to recover. I recommend a long soak in a warm bath. Shall we say—eight o'clock?'

Isobel blew out a breath. Eight o'clock! The way she was feeling, she would have preferred an early night, but at least it would be a short evening.

'That sounds good to me,' she managed, and as he made arrangements to pick her up she reflected that at least he was unlikely to hear any gossip before then.

CHAPTER TEN

JARED had initially booked a room for two nights at the Moat House Hotel in Polgarth.

He supposed he'd had some wild idea—futile, as it had turned out—that as soon as Isobel saw him again she'd fall into his arms and the booking could be cancelled. Even knowing she'd come here to find her father, he'd been confident that he could persuade her to come back.

Of course he hadn't. But he hadn't driven home that night. As his anger had cooled, so had his intellect, and he'd known that he had to see her again. He hadn't given her time to think over what he'd said, and it was possible that she'd been so shocked to see him that her reactions had been coloured by an instinctive desire to defend herself.

If she'd never found those letters and conceived this crazy notion of finding her biological father she'd never have dreamt of moving to Cornwall. He was sure of it. She might have left Newcastle: he had to accept that she'd had that in mind for some time, and, however painful it was to stomach, he had to try and understand her motives.

He spent Friday kicking his heels in Polgarth. It was a nice little town, with one or two decent hotels and a shopping precinct surrounding a central square. There was even a museum, and he spent some time examining the tools and other implements that were all that was left of the tin-mining that used to be so prevalent in the area. These days, most of the mines had closed, and, reading about the conditions the miners used to work under, Jared couldn't help but think that that was a good thing. Having been raised in the north-east of England, he was very familiar with

110

mining and its difficulties, and although people missed the
camaraderie that had existed in mining communities, there
was no doubt that they didn't miss the dangers.

It crossed his mind that he might run into Isobel in
Polgarth. He remembered she'd always used to make her
weekly visit to the supermarket on Fridays, and that
brought back memories of how they'd first met.

She'd been so mortified at reversing her car into his, he
recalled ruefully. Particularly when she'd had to confess
to being a teacher, as well. She'd admitted that she'd always impressed upon her pupils the necessity to take es-
pecial care in car parks. People often reversed out of bays
without thinking, she'd told them, and the possible consequences of her carelessness had stayed with her for
weeks.

From Jared's point of view, he'd been grateful for the
introduction. His attraction to her had seemed as natural
as breathing and he'd hated the thought of having to tell
her he was a married man. But, as it happened, he hadn't
had to. She'd recognised his name from things her sister
had said. As usual, Marion had been shamelessly social
climbing, and she had already been pretending that the
Goldmans were close friends.

To begin with, he knew, Isobel had had no intention of
becoming involved with him. She'd liked him; he'd
known that. But she'd kept their association an impersonal
one, concerned simply with arranging for her insurance
company to cover his repairs. The damage to his car had
been minimal, and he could easily have attended to it himself without involving her. But it had been a means of
keeping in touch with her, and he'd exploited it shamelessly for his own ends.

From the beginning of their association Jared had insisted that they were doing no harm. The predictable excuse of any married man, he conceded now. But when
he'd told her that he and Elizabeth were living separate

lives, he hadn't been lying. He'd assured Isobel that he was asking for her friendship, nothing more...

Jared bought a sandwich for his lunch and ate it in his car, overlooking a wooded ravine just outside of town. Then, leaving the car, he hiked down into the valley, following the course of a tumbling stream that had been swollen by recent rains.

It was a beautiful part of the country, he acknowledged, wondering why he had chosen to return to the north of England after he'd got his degree. Perhaps he'd been destined to go back to Newcastle to meet Isobel, he reflected. Flinging himself down onto a flat rock beside the stream, he raked frustrated fingers through his hair. He didn't even want to think of how he'd feel if she insisted on staying here.

He took a deep breath and stared blindly across the stream to where a few late pansies were still blooming. It was his own fault, he thought bitterly. If he'd kept his promise, she'd never have felt the need to get away. She probably thought he'd lied when he'd said that all he wanted was her friendship. Of course he'd wanted to make love with her, but to begin with just being with her had been enough.

And he hadn't made any undue demands upon her. For weeks, months, even, he'd contented himself with being in her company, sharing her humour, delighting in making her smile. From the very beginning, their relationship had not been like any other relationship he had had.

He grimaced, taking off his glasses and wearily tipping back his head. Was that entirely true? Hadn't he taken every opportunity he could to touch her? From putting his arm around her to guide her into a restaurant, to taking her hand whenever they walked together?

But she'd let him do it, he defended himself. Smiling up at him so confidently, laughing at his jokes, teasing him mercilessly. She'd even massaged his shoulders when he'd gone to her apartment with the tensions of the day still stiffening his spine. She'd done everything except kiss him, and gradually the strain had begun to tell on both of them.

Ironically enough, it had been Isobel who'd broken their self-imposed abstinence. Three years before, her mother had been diagnosed with a certain virulent form of cancer, and, although she had had surgery and chemotherapy treatment at the time, nine months ago it had reappeared.

Isobel had been devastated when the doctor had given her the news, and she'd done something she'd never done before: she'd called him on his mobile phone and begged him to come to the apartment. And when he'd arrived—barely thirty minutes later, he remembered, having broken every speed limit in the city to get to her—she'd virtually thrown herself into his arms.

Between incoherent sobs, she'd told him about her mother, and although Jared had comforted her, he'd never imagined that she wanted anything more from him than that. He'd thought he'd understood how she was feeling, but he'd been wrong. She hadn't just wanted his sympathy, she'd wanted him, wholly and completely, an affirmation of life at a time when she'd seemed surrounded by the shadows of death.

But, dammit, he didn't want to think about making love with her now; didn't want to remember how sweet that first time had been; how sweet and trusting *she* had been, offering herself to him with a complete lack of guile or artifice. God, it had been so good then, so satisfying, and that fledgling encounter had been the start of their affair.

He drove back to his hotel in the late afternoon, resisting the impulse to go to the cottage with a distinct effort. Better to wait, he told himself. Better to give her a whole day to think about what she'd said. If he went back now, she would know that he hadn't taken her seriously, and that would defeat the object.

He considered ordering his dinner from Room Service, but the idea of spending the whole evening with only himself for company didn't appeal. He hadn't bothered with dinner at all the night before, but the considerable quantity of alcohol he'd swallowed in the bar had filled the empty space inside him. Tonight, however, he had no intention of getting drunk, and watching his fellow guests couldn't be any less entertaining than staring at the four walls of his room.

The restaurant was fairly full when he went downstairs, and he was glad he'd taken the trouble to wear a jacket and tie. It was obviously a favourite place to eat for the people of Polgarth, because he didn't recognise many faces from when he'd had breakfast that morning. He guessed that most of the diners were just out for the evening, but at least he didn't feel conspicuous as he accompanied the *maître d'* to his table by the window.

Yet, for all that, he sensed his arrival had not gone unremarked. He might be flattering himself, and it was probably nothing more than the unfamiliarity of dining on his own, but after he'd been seated and the waiter had supplied him with a menu, he took a surreptitious inventory of the room.

And suffered an immediate blow to his gut.

Isobel was sitting not twenty feet away, sharing a table for two with a man he'd never seen before. But she was staring at him as if she couldn't believe the evidence of her own eyes and he could hardly blame her. She'd obviously assumed he'd returned to Newcastle, and as she hadn't known where he was staying anyway, the chances of them both dining in the same restaurant must have been hundreds to one. Although, remembering Polgarth's limitations when it came to gourmet eating, perhaps not.

His eyes consumed her. She looked so beautiful, her dark hair, which had grown in the six weeks since she'd left Newcastle, a curly halo about her face. He thought she looked pale, but that was probably just the shock she'd had upon seeing him, and as she was wearing a simple black dress, her pallor was impossibly pronounced.

The man she was with leant towards her then and said something, and Isobel dragged her eyes away to answer him. Whatever he'd said, it brought a faint smile to her lips and, seeing it, Jared knew he had to get out of there before he did something unforgivable. Already the collar of his shirt was feeling unpleasantly tight and hot colour was sweeping up his neck to darken his skin. He needed a drink, he thought savagely. Something strong and powerful, that would cut through the constriction in his throat that was threatening to strangle him.

He thrust back his chair and got to his feet, aware that by doing so he was creating exactly the spectacle he'd most wanted to avoid. The *maître d'* came hurrying towards him, evidently alarmed that the waiter had said or done something to offend him, and what with reassuring him, and avoiding the eyes of the other diners, Jared was unaware that Isobel had left her seat and come to join them.

'Jared,' she said, her low voice reaching him even over the flustered protestations of the manager, but although he could hear the anxiety in her tone, he couldn't bear to look at her.

'Go back to your friend, Isobel,' he said harshly, fighting back the urge to go and bury his fist in the other man's face, and, uncaring of what anybody thought of him now, he pushed both of them aside and strode out of the restaurant.

He couldn't wait to get out of his formal clothes, and he was already loosening the neck of his shirt and pulling his tie free of his collar as he vaulted up the stairs. God, what a fool he'd been, he berated himself bitterly. He'd believed her when she'd told him there was no one else, but it was obvious now why she'd really left town. There was no way in hell that the guy with her was her father, and she had hardly had time to get to know anyone else.

'Jared!'

She was at the foot of the stairs now, gazing up at him with an imploring expression on her face, and he thought how pitiful it was that he still wanted to give her the benefit of the doubt.

'Go away, Isobel,' he said coldly, pausing only long enough to deliver these words, and he heard the sob that marked her intake of breath.

'Jared, you don't understand.'

'You got that right,' muttered Jared to himself as he stalked along the corridor to his room. He was hurt, and he told himself his feelings were justifiable, even if the knowledge that he had no real right to blame her was gnawing at his conscience.

He had his keycard in his hand before he reached his room, and, jabbing it into the lock, he thrust the door open with enough force to ensure that the recoil slammed it shut behind him. Then, pulling off his tie and tossing it onto the bed, he walked straight across to the phone and punched out the number for Room Service.

He was waiting impatiently for someone to answer when there was a tentative tap at his door. He stiffened abruptly, but before he could abandon his call and go and answer it Room Service came on the line.

Deciding whoever was outside would have to wait, he turned his back on the door deliberately. 'I want a bottle of Scotch,' he said shortly to the woman who had responded, and after giving his room number he slammed the phone down again.

The tap at his door was repeated.

Taking a deep breath, he considered ignoring it, but the suspicion of who it was drove him across the room again. Flinging open the door, he was hardly surprised to find

Isobel outside, but he had no intention of listening to any more lies from her.

'Go away,' he said flatly, but when he would have shut the door again, she insinuated herself into the opening.

'Please, Jared—'

'Please, what?' He was in no mood to bandy words with her, and only the fact that he would have to physically man-handle her out of the doorway prevented him from accomplishing his objective. The last thing he wanted to do was lay his hands on her. He had the uneasy feeling that if he did he might not be able to let her go again. 'You're wasting your time, Isobel.'

'Isobel?' Her lips quivered at his formal use of her name. 'Please—can't we talk? I don't want you to—to go away with the wrong impression.'

'Is that possible?' Jared was sardonic, but his will was weakening, he could feel it, and, stifling a curse, he left the door and put some space between them. 'Make it quick.'

Isobel didn't say anything immediately. She simply came into the room, closing the door with more care than he'd shown, and then stood there like a schoolgirl, her hands, one on top of the other, forming a horizontal line at the apex of her thighs.

Jared's jacket joined his tie on the bed and he turned to face her, arms crossed at his midriff. He didn't want to feel any sympathy for her, but he couldn't help noticing that she was paler even than before.

Yet she seemed to have gained a little weight, he observed sourly, wondering if it was the natural result of several weeks without work or because she no longer had to live with the stress of their relationship. Whatever, it suited her, and he had to drag his eyes away from the unknowingly provocative thrust of her breasts.

But he could feel himself hardening, and, in an effort

to keep her off-guard, he arched a mocking brow. 'Is he good?'

Isobel's gasp was pained. 'How can you ask something like that?'

Jared shrugged. 'Well, I can't imagine what else you have to tell me. I just wish you'd been honest when I came to the cottage. It would have saved me from kicking my heels around here for the last twenty-four hours.'

'So, why did you?' she protested unsteadily. 'Stay here, I mean? I—I thought you must have gone back to Newcastle.'

'Hoped,' Jared corrected her caustically. 'The word you're looking for is 'hoped'. You *hoped* I'd gone back to Newcastle, didn't you?'

'I—yes.' Her momentary hesitation was no recompense. 'Of course I hoped you'd gone back. We—we'd said all there was to say. Hadn't we?'

'So what are you doing here, then?'

She shook her head, as if he'd disappointed her. 'You know what I'm doing here,' she insisted. 'I don't want you to think—to imagine that Luke and I—'

'Luke?' His lips curled.

'Yes, Luke. Luke Herrington,' she said defensively. 'He's my landlord. He owns the cottage I'm renting.' She gestured behind her. 'This—this evening was intended to be a kind of celebration of me moving in.'

'Oh, yeah, right.'

It was obvious that he didn't believe her, and Isobel spread her hands in helpless appeal. 'It's the truth.' She gazed at him entreatingly. 'Why would I lie to you?'

'I can think of a number of reasons,' he retorted bitterly. 'Like, you've thought I was a bastard for so long, you wouldn't want to lose your advantage.'

Isobel's lips parted. '*I* thought you were a bastard?'

'You said it.'

She left the door and came towards him. 'I don't know

what the hell you're talking about,' she got out chokingly. She swallowed, her throat working convulsively. 'I—I have never—never thought you were—' She couldn't seem to say it. 'I—I loved you, Jared.'

'Loved?' His contempt was audible. 'What is love? I don't know, and I doubt it to hell that you do either. What is this? Some kind of guilt trip? D'you expect me to believe you left me because you loved me? Come on, Isobel. I've been down this path before.'

'And I'm not Elizabeth,' said Isobel fiercely, moving her head agitatedly from side to side. 'Why are you saying these things, Jared? Can't we at least part as friends?'

'I'm not your friend,' snarled Jared, hardly knowing what he was saying, and, uncaring of the hands she raised to stop him, he jerked her into his arms. His mouth fastened on hers, taking advantage of her parted lips, and he thrust his tongue hungrily between her teeth.

He knew the moment she stopped fighting him. Her hands, which had curled into fists at his midriff, opened and spread against the fine fabric of his shirt. Her breasts flattened against his chest, and as she arched against him his arousal was cushioned by the womanly softness of her stomach.

'God, Belle,' he groaned, releasing her mouth to seek the scented hollow of her neck, and, almost against her will, it seemed, her hands curved up to pull off his glasses and bring his mouth back to hers.

He was hungry for the taste of her, for the feel of her warm body in his arms. He wanted to touch every part of her, to strip away the barriers of their clothes that separated them and enclose her securely within the possessive circle of his embrace.

His hands slid down the slender column of her spine to the rounded swell of her bottom and brought her even closer to his aching loins. Hiking up the silky skirt of her dress, he wedged one leg between the sensual heat of her thighs. She was wearing black stockings, and above their lacy tops sexy suspenders gave a tantalising glimpse of pale flesh.

Jared's breathing quickened in concert with the accelerated beat of his heart. Opening her mouth wider, to give him greater access to the moist cavern within, he nibbled at the sensitive softness of her inner flesh, biting the provocative curl of her tongue when it came to duel with his.

Her mouth was so hot, so sweet, so familiar, and his senses reeled beneath the onslaught of so many dizzying sensations. She'd thrown his glasses onto the bed and her hands were in his hair, her nails raking his scalp, sliding into the collar of his shirt, loosening buttons to expose his hair-roughened chest.

His erection throbbed painfully, eager for release, eager to bury itself in the wet curls that pulsed against his leg. Desire, like a ravening beast, blinded him to everything but the consummation of his own needs. He wanted her; ah, God, she was as important to his survival as the air he breathed, and somehow he had to convince her of that.

He'd forgotten about the man downstairs, the man she'd been having dinner with. He'd forgotten the betrayal he'd felt when he'd seen them together, or how much he'd despised himself for his own selfishness in not wanting to let her go. Right now, the idea that this woman, *his* woman, might be operating under a different agenda from his own didn't even occur to him. He'd even forgotten where they were, and why he was here, miles from everything that was familiar to him. All his bemused brain was telling him was that Isobel was here, they were together, and soon, very soon, he was going to feel her responsive flesh opening to his. Her muscles, those tight demanding muscles, would close around him, and his aching body would find its release in the sensual sweetness of hers.

His guard was down, he was briefly vulnerable, and when someone knocked at the door it took him a few precious seconds to comprehend its significance. Precious seconds that Isobel used to her advantage. With a groan, she thrust him away from her; thrust him away with such force that the backs of his knees hit the edge of the bed and he toppled helplessly onto the mattress, only narrowly avoiding crushing his glasses.

He rebounded at once, the shock instantly rousing him from the mindless confusion his senses had created. But it was too late. Isobel had already reached the door and was pulling it open, and any chance of grabbing her and trying to regain the advantage was thwarted by the appearance of the hotel waiter with the Scotch he'd ordered earlier.

'Your whisky, sir,' said the man politely, but Jared could tell from his expression that he wasn't unaware of what had been going on before he knocked at the door. Even without his glasses Jared could see that Isobel's mouth was swollen, and there were creases in her skirt that hadn't been there before. Besides which, his shirt was unbuttoned almost to his waist, and, although his erection had subsided, his own frustration must have been unmistakable.

'Goodbye, Jared.'

Evidently, Isobel felt obliged to say something to try and normalise the situation, and, uncaring what the man thought, Jared bounded across the room and caught her arm as she was hurrying away along the corridor.

'Wait!'

'I can't.'

She was stiff now, her face pale and unyielding, and Jared's teeth ground together. 'Dammit, you can't go like this,' he muttered, conscious of the waiter behind him. 'Please, Belle: I won't touch you if you don't want me to, but come back into the room.'

'No.' She looked down at his fingers gripping her arm, and with a muffled oath he released her, knowing he wasn't aiding his case by holding her against her will. 'Luke will be wondering where I am.'

Jared was tempted to say, To hell with Luke, but he had the sense to realise that losing his temper was unlikely to achieve anything either. Instead, with enforced patience, he said, 'He can wait a few minutes longer.'

'No, he can't.' She was determined not to compromise with him. 'I should never have come up here. I don't know why I did, really, except that—that—'

'You couldn't help yourself?' he suggested huskily, but she turned her head away.

'I was going to say that I—felt I owed you an explanation,' she responded. 'I should have known better.' Her lips twisted bitterly. 'I should have realised you'd take any advantage and use it to your own ends.'

'They were your ends too.'

'Not any more.' She glanced at him with tormented eyes. 'I've tried to tell you I don't know how many times, Jared. We're finished. It's over. I'll get over it. So will you. And we'll both get over it a whole lot sooner if you stop trying to rekindle a dying fire.'

'This—is—not—a—dying—fire,' he enunciated harshly, but when he would have grasped her hands, she thrust them behind her back.

'It is. Accept it, Jared, and go home. Please. I don't know why you're still here, but if you're planning on visiting the cottage again, forget it. I won't answer the door.'

CHAPTER ELEVEN

IT WAS raining again.

Having forced herself to crawl out of bed when the alarm rang for the second time, Isobel crossed to the window and gazed out at the overcast skies with weary resignation. It seemed to have done nothing but rain since she started work and she was heartily sick of it.

Sick of everything, herself included, she acknowledged miserably, padding into the bathroom. Why had she ever thought that making a fresh start would give her life new meaning? Sometimes it was even hard to remember what her motivation for coming to Polgarron had been, and the idea of making some contact with the Dorlands of Tregarth Hall grew more unlikely with every passing day.

She had successfully severed her relationship with Jared, of course, even if the advantages of that were sometimes equally hard to justify. Which was stupid, she reminded herself now, viewing the reflection of her steadily burgeoning stomach in the mirror above the washbasin. There was no way she could have allowed Jared to find out about the baby. He wanted her, but he didn't love her. He'd made that painfully clear. And the fact that he and Elizabeth had never had any children must surely prove that they were not on his agenda either.

She shivered. It was definitely getting colder in the mornings, and already she was missing the benefits of central heating. Perhaps she could suggest to Luke that radiators were no longer considered a luxury, she considered. Though, since she'd told him she was expecting a baby, his interest in his new tenant had seriously waned.

So long as he didn't cancel her lease, she could live

with it, she thought wryly. At least until the baby was born, anyway. So far, she hadn't considered what she was going to do afterwards. There was no doubt she was missing her friends and family more than she could have imagined, the long phone conversations she had with Michelle only partly compensating for the gulf there was between them.

Between you and Jared, you mean. Her hormones kicked in grumpily, and she felt the familiar pull of tears. Despite all the warnings she had given herself, she still thought about him—a lot. Every time the baby moved, every time she noticed some new change in her body, she wanted to share it with him, and it was agony knowing she never could.

If she occasionally felt a pang of guilt at keeping her condition a secret from him, she quelled it. But there were still nights when she lay awake for hours on end, the knowledge of her own duplicity an inescapable burden.

Perhaps if she'd made some contact with the Dorlands it would have been easier for her, she conceded. She had wondered if the Dorlands themselves might show some interest in her, but so far their paths hadn't crossed. She didn't even know if they knew that another person of the same name was living in the village. From what little she had gathered, they didn't mix much with the local people.

She wished there was someone she could ask about them, but she was afraid of appearing too nosy. The snippets she had learned she'd gleaned from Joanne James, who also worked at the school where she was supply-teaching at present. Joanne was the school secretary, and although it had been natural enough during their early conversations for Isobel to comment on the fact that she'd heard there were other Dorlands living in the village, she'd realised that any subsequent interest in them was bound to arouse Joanne's curiosity.

The water was only lukewarm, so Isobel didn't linger

long in the bathroom. At least the sense of nausea had left her, she thought gratefully. She would have hated to have to deal with that as well in her current state of depression.

Then, she had the frustrating task of finding something to wear that didn't overtly advertise her condition. So far, she'd managed to get away with loose-fitting dresses, but it was getting too cold for summer clothes, and her winter clothes were much too tight.

She really would have to make an effort and go into Polgarth at the weekend, she conceded unwillingly. It would be October next week, and, just because she hadn't a lot of interest in her appearance at the moment, that was no reason to go round looking like a frump. She needed some maternity clothes, and no one else was going to buy them for her.

Rummaging through the drawers, she discovered a cream sweater that she'd once borrowed from Jared and never returned. It was big and bulky, the long sleeves falling over her hands so that she had to keep pushing them up over her forearms. But it was warm, and comforting, and teamed with a wrap-around navy skirt it looked pretty good.

She lit the fire in the living room while the kettle was boiling. It wasn't that she had much time to benefit from it before she went to work, but it made the cottage warm and cosy for when she came home. In fact, it was the one aspect of living in the cottage that she really appreciated. It was years since she'd enjoyed the advantages of an open fire.

The school where she had a temporary teaching position was in the nearby village of Rose Cross. Rose Cross was a much bigger village than Polgarron, and the secondary school catered to the needs of the children from all the surrounding villages. Isobel was helping out because a member of the English department was just recovering from a serious operation, and she expected to stay there until Christmas, at least.

Which meant she was unlikely to need another post until after the baby was born. The date she'd been given, of the middle of January, seemed fairly definite according to Dr Wilson, whose practice was in Rose Cross, too. Joanne had said the doctor who'd used to have a surgery in Polgarron had retired, and it was convenient to fit in her appointments after school was over for the day.

Of course, Isobel had had to visit the hospital in Polgarth for her scan, which had taken place a few weeks ago. Michelle had pressed her not to put off the examination, and she'd been relieved to find she wouldn't have to go to St Austell when the baby was due.

But it had been another stage of her pregnancy that she would have liked to have shared with Jared, she reflected now, as she got into her car. She'd chosen not to be told the baby's sex, but she had learned that he—or she—was perfectly normal, and once again her hand curved possessively over her womb.

She usually stopped at the stores before driving out of the village. Mrs Scott, who owned the stores and ran the post office, also supplied newspapers and magazines, and Isobel had started to collect a paper on her way to work. It made her feel more like a local, despite her sense of alienation, and Mrs Scott never failed to ask how she was when she came in.

There was another woman in the shop this morning, a tall young woman, with hair as dark as her own, who was apparently complaining about a magazine that hadn't been delivered. Her voice, an unusually arrogant voice, Isobel noticed, was raised in protest, and she glanced round impatiently when Isobel came into the shop.

'Morning, Ms Dorland,' called Mrs Scott cheerfully, before resuming her attempt to pacify the girl. But the young woman had heard Isobel's name and turned again to regard her with suspicious eyes.

'Your name's Dorland?' she enquired, as if she had every right to ask the question, and Isobel felt herself stiffening.

'Just the *Mail*, Mrs Scott,' she said, without answering her, handing over the necessary change. 'Thanks.'

She was obviously going to leave without speaking to the girl, and, as if she felt obliged to say something in mitigation, Mrs Scott hurriedly intervened. 'Er—this young lady is called Dorland, too,' she said, with an appealing look at Isobel. 'You may have heard of Mrs Dorland of Tregarth Hall?'

Isobel's jaw dropped. 'You're Mrs Dorland?' she said faintly, and the young woman tossed Mrs Scott a disparaging look.

'Of course not,' she exclaimed scornfully, but it was hardly a reassurance. 'I'm Barbara Dorland. Her daughter.'

Her *daughter*!

So, it was true, then. Robert Dorland had been lying when he'd told his sister-in-law that his wife couldn't have children. This girl was proof of it, and Isobel wondered why the news didn't come as any surprise to her.

'Well—I'd better be going,' she began, but Barbara Dorland had another question.

'You don't know my mother, do you?' she probed, and despite herself Isobel felt the colour draining out of her cheeks.

'No,' she said quickly, reaching for the handle of the door, but Barbara still wasn't finished with her.

'You don't come from around here, do you?' she persisted. 'Are you staying in the village?'

'Ms Dorland's renting Raven Cottage,' put in Mrs Scott, before Isobel could stop her. She smiled beneficently. 'Barbara's just got back from the United States,' she added to Isobel, as if to even the score.

'How nice.' Isobel found it difficult to be friendly towards the young woman, but, reminding herself that her feelings had nothing to do with Barbara, she forced a smile. 'Well—'

'Does your—er—husband work in Polgarth?' The girl's eyes were moving assessingly over Isobel's thickening waistline now, but once again it was Mrs Scott who answered her.

'Ms Dorland's partner isn't living with her at present,' she declared firmly, giving Isobel an encouraging smile. 'And we mustn't keep her or she'll be late for work.'

'You're still working?'

Barbara made it sound incredibly foolish, and Isobel wondered if it was just jealousy that made her want to slap the other woman's face. 'Some of us have to,' she remarked, guessing from the designer cut of Barbara Dorland's clothes that she wasn't one of them. 'Bye.'

She was shaking when she got back into her car, and she couldn't decide if it was the shock of meeting her half-sister or simple anger at Barbara's obvious insensitivity.

Michelle rang that evening.

'Hey, how're you doing, kid?' she asked cheerfully, and instantly sensed from Isobel's tone that something was up. 'Have I rung at the wrong time?'

'As if.' Isobel's voice was a little gruff. 'No, I'm fine. How about you?'

'Same old, same old,' said Michelle ruefully. 'What can I tell you? Oh, yeah. Mr Seton's excluded Wayne Harris for the second time, and Karen Weaver is pregnant.'

'Pregnant!' Isobel forgot her own problems for a moment in the familiar politics of her old school. 'I bet her father's pleased about that!'

'He's spitting blood, I can tell you.' Michelle chuckled. 'Particularly as Karen's mother is insisting that Karen should be allowed to decide if she wants to have the baby or not.'

'And the fact that Mr Weaver has custody doesn't have anything to do with it, I suppose,' remarked Isobel drily. 'So what's going to happen?'

'Your guess is as good as mine.' Michelle snorted. 'If Social Services have their way, she'll probably be encouraged to have the baby and then have it adopted. I think that's the current philosophy. Naturally, Karen's father was hoping for a termination.'

'He would be.'

Isobel sounded wistful, and Michelle picked up on her uncertainty. 'Hey, you're not having second thoughts about having your baby, are you?'

'No.' Isobel was vehement. 'That's one thing I've got no doubts about.'

'So what's that supposed to mean?' Michelle hesitated. 'Help me out here, Issy. Do I take it you're still having doubts about breaking up with Jared?'

'No.' But Isobel sounded less convinced of that. 'I—I was talking to Barbara Dorland today,' she added, with some reluctance.

'Barbara Dorland?' Michelle was startled. 'I thought you said your aunt's name was Justine?'

'It was. It is.' Isobel sighed. 'Barbara's her daughter.'

'My God!' Michelle's gulp was audible. 'I see.'

Isobel sighed again. 'I thought you would.'

'I gather you still haven't told them who you are?'

'No.'

'Are you going to?'

'I don't know.' Isobel was resigned. 'I keep telling myself that—that if he'd wanted to speak to me, he'd have made some overture before now.'

'There is that.' Michelle obviously sympathised. 'So what did she say?'

'Barbara?' Isobel was thoughtful. 'Not a lot. But she was obviously curious about me.'

'Was she?'

'Yes, but not the way you think.' Isobel paused, and then explained, 'She was in the shop when I called for my paper this morning. She heard Mrs Scott call me Ms *Dorland*, and she must have thought that gave her the right to ask me all sorts of questions.'

'What questions?'

'Oh—' Isobel tried to think. 'Well, she asked if I knew her mother, for one thing. And then she asked if I came from this area, and so on. Oh, and she asked if my husband worked in Polgarth.'

'Your *husband*?' Michelle gave a short incredulous laugh. 'That was pretty nosy, wasn't it?'

'I thought so.' Isobel tried to sound indignant, but her anxiety was showing again. 'I think she noticed—that I was pregnant, I mean.'

'Ah.' Michelle was beginning to understand. 'And you're afraid she may tell her father?'

'Something like that.'

'Well, what does it matter? He was bound to find out sooner or later.'

'I know.'

'Issy, don't let these people get to you. Okay, I guess finding out that you've possibly got half-sisters and brothers is upsetting, but you don't have to stay there. You know that. You could move somewhere else.'

'Yeah, right.'

'I mean it.' Michelle sighed now. 'Look, why don't you take a break? Come up here for a few days. You can stay with us. No one need know you're here if you don't want them to. And you don't have to worry about meeting Jared because he's away.'

Isobel gasped. 'Away?' she echoed weakly, not realising until that moment that, in spite of everything, she still relied on the fact that, if she really needed him, he was just at the end of a phone line.

'Yeah.' Michelle seemed to regret having mentioned it

now, but she had no choice but to go on. 'They've all gone away. Mr Goldman; Elizabeth; Jared; oh, and that physiotherapist Elizabeth seems to think so highly of.'

Isobel swallowed. 'What do you mean—gone away?'

'As in, on holiday,' explained Michelle reluctantly. 'I wouldn't have known myself if I hadn't seen Marion in town a couple of nights ago. I'm surprised she hasn't rung and told you all about it. That's the sort of thing she usually does, isn't it?'

Isobel stifled a groan. It was possible that Marion had rung the day before. The phone had been ringing when she got in from work, but she'd been too late to answer it.

But now she said, 'So—where've they gone?' endeavouring not to sound as devastated as she felt.

'Would you believe on a cruise?' Michelle attempted a sardonic laugh. 'Not Jared's cup of tea, I'd have thought, but Elizabeth will be lapping it up. A swish stateroom; dining at the Captain's table! Just what the doctor ordered.'

Isobel wet her dry lips. 'Isn't it a bit late in the season to be going on a cruise?'

'Hey, people go cruising all the year round. And it's still pretty warm around the Mediterranean.' Michelle paused. 'Anyway, what about you taking a holiday? Doesn't a few days in the old place have any appeal?'

It did, more than Isobel cared to admit, and the prospect of getting away from the cottage for a few days was irresistibly appealing.

'How can I?' she asked now. 'I've only been working at Rose Cross for a little over three weeks. I can't leave them in the lurch.'

'There's always the weekend,' pointed out Michelle, undeterred. 'Surely that old car of yours can make the journey. Come up on Friday evening and go back Sunday. What do you say?'

CHAPTER TWELVE

Jared got back from London on Friday evening.

The house was quiet when he let himself into the hall and he breathed a sigh of relief. For the next week, at least, he would have the place to himself, and he welcomed the prospect. With Elizabeth and Janet away, he'd have time to think, to plan; to decide what in hell he was going to do with his life.

Since coming back from Cornwall he'd been bitter and unsettled. He'd been forced to reappraise his future, and he didn't like what he'd found. He'd been drifting; he realised that now. For the past three years he'd been living a life in limbo, and he'd been selfish enough to expect Isobel to share it with him.

No wonder she'd cut him out of her life. No wonder she'd taken the first opportunity to move away. He believed her when she said she wanted a real relationship, a real family. Dammit, wasn't that what he'd wanted before he'd managed to screw everything up?

He tossed his jacket over the banister, and, switching on lamps as he went, he crossed the hall and entered the steel and chrome sophistication of the kitchen. A strip of angled spotlights lit up the various working surfaces, but Jared had always thought the place had a clinical appearance. It wasn't his design, and he entered it only infrequently these days. Howard had insisted on employing a housekeeper after Elizabeth's accident, and Mrs Webster kept it gleaming like a new pin.

Now, however, the housekeeper was away, too. Elizabeth had insisted that Mrs Webster deserved a holiday as well, but if she'd hoped that threatening him with having to look after himself would make him change his mind about accompanying them on the cruise, she'd been mistaken.

Jared had already had it out with Howard, and, although he'd been sorry to disappoint the older man, his threats no longer held any fears either. He'd reached the point where he didn't much care what happened in the future, and he suspected Howard had realised that, and that was why he'd backed off.

In the event, it had been Howard who'd eventually justified Jared's reasons for staying in England. Despite the unlikelihood of them being offered the contract, his father-in-law had decided that they should tender for a proposed development at Spitalfields. Which was why Jared had spent the first week they were away in London, viewing the site and holding meetings with the various authorities, and making preliminary drawings in his hotel room at night.

They'd all flown to Heathrow together. Then Howard and the two women had flown on to Malta, to rendezvous with the ship, and Jared had taken a taxi into town.

It had been a fairly hectic week and he'd met some interesting people, but he couldn't deny he was glad to be back. He still hoped that Isobel might have had a change of heart, and he intended to speak to Michelle Chambers if he could.

Crazy? He grimaced. Perhaps, but he was desperate. Despite the fact that he could fill his days with work, he couldn't keep Isobel out of his thoughts when he went to bed. He tortured himself wondering where she might be and what she was doing. And, more agonising still, who she might be with.

He'd tried to tell himself that he didn't believe she was involved with Herrington. Although he couldn't forget what he'd seen at the hotel in Polgarth, his inner self rejected the interpretation he'd made. Isobel wasn't like

Elizabeth; she didn't lie to save her own face. But if she was serious about ending their relationship—and he had to believe she was—he wanted her to know exactly what it was she was giving up.

If she didn't already know, he chided himself contemptuously. His lips twisted. He was fooling himself if he thought he could salvage anything worthwhile from this mess. She despised him now for taking advantage of her without offering her any commitment. He had to tell her he was sorry. He had to ask her to forgive him.

Filling the coffee pot with water, he left it to filter through the beans he'd ground while he made himself an omelette. He wasn't particularly hungry, but, as he hadn't had anything since a slice of toast that morning at the hotel, he knew he had to eat something.

There was no fresh bread in the house, but he would worry about that in morning. For the present, the eggs would do, and, after pouring himself a mug of black coffee, he set the meal on a tray and carried it through to his study at the back of the house.

The message light on the answering machine was winking at him, and although he told himself that it could wait until morning, too, the unlikely thought that it could be something urgent forced him to press the button.

As he'd expected, all the calls were business-related. Even the invitations from other firms and colleagues to social events were all slanted towards his position at Goldman Lewis, and with an exclamation of disgust he switched the machine off. Dammit, that was what his life had become and he was sick of it. It was time to tell Elizabeth he wanted out.

Michelle Chambers and her husband lived in the Fenham district of the city.

According to Isobel, she and Michelle had known one another since their schooldays, when they'd both lived near Jesmond Dene, and, although they'd lost touch with one another afterwards, they'd met up again teaching at the same school. Jared knew her only slightly, but he was well aware that Michelle didn't approve of him. A situation that he hoped to reverse. He needed her help, not her condemnation, however well deserved it might be.

He knew where Michelle lived. He'd passed the house a couple of times since Isobel went away, originally in the hope of seeing Michelle and begging her to tell him where her friend had gone. He'd even spoken to her on the phone on one abortive occasion, when she'd told him in no uncertain terms that if Isobel wanted him to know where she was, she'd tell him herself.

Which had been fair enough, he supposed honestly. And, in the event, he'd managed to find Isobel without her help. But now he wanted something different from her: he wanted to know if Isobel was seeing anyone else. If Michelle thought he had any chance of persuading her to come back to him.

As if she'd tell him.

But he had to try.

He saw the little grey Fiesta the minute he turned into Cunningham Grove. It wasn't a large cul-de-sac, and the Chambers' house was situated at the end, in full view of anyone who turned off the main thoroughfare. And there was Isobel's car, parked neatly at the gate.

His foot found the brake almost involuntarily, and he swung jerkily into the kerb, narrowly avoiding a bicycle that was parked there. But the shock of seeing her car, of knowing that Isobel had come back, was so shattering that he needed a few minutes to recover his scattered senses.

When had she decided to return to Newcastle? he wondered. When had she changed her mind about making a life for herself so far from all the people and places she knew and loved? And why hadn't she told him?

The answer was obvious, of course. As his heartbeat

slowed and the trickle of perspiration that had dampened his temples dried, he realised he had no grounds for thinking she'd changed her mind. Quite the opposite, in fact. It wasn't a coincidence that Isobel had chosen to visit Michelle this weekend when everyone no doubt assumed he was away with his wife and her father. Isobel's sister could have told her. Elizabeth was bound to have mentioned the cruise at the golf club. The last thing she'd be expecting was for him to turn up.

He blew out a breath. Now what? Could he really walk up to Michelle's door and ask to speak to her? Would she be prepared to speak to him?

Of course, Michelle might not let him in. And, judging by the cars parked in the drive, her husband was home as well. Not that he was daunted by the thought of facing Phil Chambers. On the contrary, he had the feeling that only another man might understand the torment he was going through.

A spatter of rain wet the windscreen of the Mercedes, and he expelled an impatient sigh. He couldn't sit here contemplating his alternatives indefinitely. Already the people who lived in the house nearby were peering out of the window, speculating as to his intentions.

Dammit, he was going to have to take a chance on her not rejecting him outright, he decided at last. He had to convince her that seeing her with Luke Herrington had made him realise how much she meant to him. Only if he saw her again would he know whether he was wasting his time.

Despite the obvious disapproval of the neighbours, Jared decided to leave the car where it was. He told himself it was because there were already too many cars parked around the Chambers' house as it was, but in fact he felt less conspicuous on foot.

He was wearing a long overcoat over black jeans and a purple tee shirt, and he pushed his hands into the coat's pockets to hold the sides together after locking the car. It was cold, damn cold, and the wind whistling between the houses didn't help. But, once again, his body heat was rising. He felt like a schoolboy, he thought mockingly, preparing to ask for a first date.

The rain blurred his vision, and he took off his glasses and rubbed them on his sleeve. But as he put them on again he saw that the front door of the Chambers' house was opening, and his pulse accelerated as Isobel and Michelle came out.

He was approximately fifty yards from the gate when Isobel saw him. He knew the moment she recognised him, because she half turned around, and he was afraid she was going to dart back into the house. Michelle hadn't seen him yet, and, judging by the fact that she was closing the door behind her, the two women were going out together. Shopping, probably, Jared speculated. He just wanted to stop and stare at Isobel, but he knew if they reached her car before he did, his chance would be lost.

But that didn't stop him gazing at her, drinking in the delightful picture she made in a long, loose-fitting coat he hadn't seen before. It was a deep blue and complemented the silky darkness of her hair. She looked well, he thought enviously, half resenting the connotations that implied. She was making a life for herself without him, and he had no real right to interfere with that.

Except...

Except that he *needed* her, he acknowledged, in a moment of self-revelation. He needed her, and if that was selfish then so be it, but he was going to do everything in his power to get her back. Elizabeth didn't need him, she'd proved that in a hundred different ways, and three years was surely a long enough penance for the sin of not caring enough.

He was well aware that if he and Elizabeth got a divorce he'd have to leave Goldman-Lewis. Howard would probably never forgive him for abandoning his daughter, and, unless Elizabeth chose to tell her father about the abortion, that would be another cross he'd have to bear. But it was a price he was prepared to pay for his freedom. Being with Isobel was the only thing that mattered to him and he was a fool for not realising it before now.

Something about Isobel's attitude must have communicated itself to her friend because Michelle frowned and turned to look in his direction. Her face changed when she saw him, whatever she'd been saying to Isobel was silenced, and they both gazed at him with guarded eyes when he halted at the foot of the drive.

'What do you want—?' Michelle started, but Jared looked only at Isobel.

'Hi,' he said, aware that his voice was gravelly with emotion. 'Can we talk?'

'You've got a nerve!' protested Michelle fiercely, stepping in front of Isobel as if there was some danger of him using force to gain his own ends.

'It's all right, Michelle.' Isobel's face had paled slightly at his appearance, but now she moved round the other woman to fix him with an unfriendly stare. 'She's right,' she added tersely. 'You have got a nerve coming here. Aren't you supposed to be cruising the Mediterranean with your wife?'

'Is that what you thought?' Jared's glasses were becoming smeared with rain again, and he pulled them off to gaze at her with hungry eyes. He was aware of Michelle getting ready to answer the question and hurried on, regardless, 'No. I've been in London; working. I just got back last night.'

'But Elizabeth—?'

'She's still away,' said Jared impatiently, not wanting to get into a discussion of his wife's whereabouts with Michelle waiting to pounce like a rabid dog. 'Look, I mean it, Belle. I would like to talk to you—alone.'

'How did you know I was here?'

Despite her friend's frustration, Isobel was evidently curious enough to ask the question, and Jared took some heart from that. 'I didn't—' he began earnestly, only to have Michelle break in again.

'If you believe that, you'll believe anything,' she said disparagingly. 'Why else do you think he's turned up?' She grimaced. 'Like the proverbial bad penny!'

Jared ignored her. 'I didn't know you were here,' he insisted, clenching his teeth when once again Michelle insisted on having her say.

'Who told you?' she demanded. 'Was it Isobel's sister? I'm surprised she's even speaking to you after—'

'No one told me.' Jared kept his temper with an effort, but, realising he had to convince Michelle of that, he turned to look at her instead. 'Can you honestly see Marion Rimmer telling me anything?'

Michelle scowled. 'So what are you saying? That you were coming to see me?' Her scepticism was evident.

'Obviously,' replied Jared flatly. 'I don't know anyone else in Cunningham Grove. You can believe it or not, I don't particularly care, but I was going to ask you if—if Isobel was—all right.'

Well, in a manner of speaking, he defended himself silently, watching Michelle's expression as she absorbed his words. Then Isobel spoke again, and he forgot all about her companion, his eyes devouring the delicate beauty of her face.

'I—' she began, and then halted for a moment. 'As you can see, I'm perfectly all right. I—appreciate your concern, but it really wasn't necessary.'

'It is necessary.' Jared spoke urgently, and then, afraid he was jeopardising his case, he forced himself to calm down. 'Belle, please—I really do want to speak with you.'

'Well, she doesn't want to talk to you,' retorted Michelle, urging her friend towards the Peugeot that was parked in the drive, and Jared's hands balled into impotent fists in his pockets.

'Wait—' To his astonishment, he saw that Isobel was holding back now. But, although he knew a moment's exultation, her next words dashed his fledgling hopes. 'You're wasting your time, Jared. I thought I'd made that perfectly plain when—when—well, weeks ago, anyway.'

'You don't understand—'

'It's you who doesn't understand,' exclaimed Michelle impatiently. 'Tell me, what part of the word "no" don't you comprehend?'

'I suggest you keep out of this,' said Jared coldly, stung into an unwary retort, and Michelle gave Isobel a triumphant look.

'You see—' she began, and Jared closed his eyes for a moment against the smugness of her expression. Then, with a gesture of defeat, he turned away, striding back towards his car before the bitterness inside him consumed his common sense.

He had the key fob in his hand, already using the remote to deactivate the alarm, when he heard Isobel calling him. Looking back over his shoulder, he saw her hurrying towards him, but although his spirits stirred in reluctant response, he had more sense than to be fooled again.

Nevertheless, he didn't attempt to get into the car, and her footsteps slowed when she realised he wasn't about to drive away. Glancing beyond her, Jared saw to his relief that Michelle had apparently gone back into the house and he supposed he ought to be thankful for small mercies.

Isobel's cheeks were flushed when she reached him and, for a woman as slim as she was, she was surprisingly out of breath. But that wasn't his concern at the moment. Even if he desperately wanted to have the right to take care of her, he hadn't yet earned her trust.

'What do you want to say?' she asked, gazing up at him

with parted lips, and he had to steel himself against the desire to cover her mouth with his own.

'We can't talk here,' he protested, glancing up the Grove, and Isobel sighed.

'Let's get into the car, then,' she said, and Jared expelled an exasperated breath.

'You are aware that we're under observation, aren't you?' he exclaimed, his eyes darting towards the house nearby, and the colour in Isobel's cheeks deepened as she realised they were being watched by an old man in a cardigan, who was standing belligerently in the bay window.

'Oh,' she said, drawing her lower lip between her teeth. 'I see what you mean.' She hesitated. 'Do you want to come up to Michelle's?'

Jared gave her a retiring look. 'Oh, right. Let's make the odds even more uneven than they were before.'

'Michelle was only sticking up for me,' said Isobel defensively. 'She thought she was doing the right thing.'

Jared's eyes darkened. 'And she wasn't?'

'No.' Isobel swallowed. 'Yes, I think she probably was. But—well, I thought I owed you—'

'Owed me?'

'Owed you a chance to explain what you think we have to say to one another,' Isobel finished firmly. And, when his mouth took on a bitter slant, 'Don't make me regret it.'

Jared breathed heavily. 'So what do you suggest we do?' He turned one hand up to the rain. 'Not exactly the weather for walking, is it?'

'No.' Isobel hesitated. 'I suppose we could—drive somewhere else.'

'We could.' Jared waited for her to say something more, and when she didn't he walked round the car and opened the passenger door. 'D'you want to get in?'

Isobel was evidently torn, but, after a rueful glance towards the Chambers' house, she seemed to come to a decision. Folding the skirt of her coat about her legs, she stepped into the vehicle.

Jared slammed the door behind her with a feeling not unlike amazement. When he'd walked away from her and Michelle a few minutes ago, he'd had no inkling that she might change her mind and come after him, and it was hard to keep his excitement under control. But he shouldn't build his hopes up, he warned himself severely. She'd made no promises; only that she was prepared to hear what he had to say.

He got behind the wheel and put the powerful car into reverse before he spoke again. 'Where are we going?'

Isobel gave him a sidelong glance. 'Where do you suggest?'

Jared quelled the impulse to tell her where he'd like to take her, and said instead, 'Somewhere quiet, I guess.' He considered. 'How about the coast?'

'The coast?' She wasn't enthusiastic. 'Can't we go to a café or somewhere close by?'

A café? Jared suppressed a groan. 'What about a pub?' he asked unhopefully, and, after a moment's hesitation, she agreed.

It wasn't his choice, but Jared contented himself with choosing a secluded hostelry on the Chollerford road, where, at this time of the morning, they could be sure of finding a quiet corner.

He led the way into the cosy bar, where a real log fire was burning, but when he asked if Isobel wanted white wine, which was her usual tipple, she shook her head.

'Just a coffee,' she said tightly, leaving him to make the order, and when he'd done so he found she'd chosen a table near the hearth, in full view of everyone who came in.

'Aren't you going to be hot here?' he asked, and she looked up at him with cool derision in her eyes.

'Don't you mean that this table is too public for you?'

she suggested, and without another word he pulled out a plush-covered armchair and sat down. 'What did you order?'

'Well, nothing alcoholic,' he assured her, checking his watch. 'How long have I got?'

Isobel gave him a defensive look. 'That's not funny.'

'Isn't it?' Jared took a deep breath. 'No, perhaps not. Okay, so—how have you been?'

'Fine.' She was abrupt. 'And you?'

Jared's lips twisted. 'Bloody awful, if you must know.'

She stiffened. 'I don't want to hear this, Jared.'

'Don't you?' Once again he filled his lungs with air in an effort to calm his nerves. 'Sorry.'

'Jared—'

'Okay, okay.'

The bartender appeared at that moment, carrying the coffee his wife had prepared for them, and while he set the tray on the table and commented about the weather, Isobel remained silent. But as soon as the man had gone again she continued her attack.

'I don't know why you're doing this, Jared,' she protested. 'Just because Elizabeth is away, and you feel free to—'

Jared swore then. 'Is that what you think?' he demanded, interrupting her. 'Is that why you think I'm here? Because Elizabeth and her father are away?'

'Well, isn't it?'

'No, dammit, it's not.' He was indignant.

'If you say so.' But she obviously didn't believe him. Had he really treated her so badly that she hated him now?

'Do you want to hear what I have to say or not?' he asked huskily, and was heartened somewhat by the fact that when she poured herself a cup of coffee, her hand shook.

'Why not?' she said at last, and he expelled the breath he had hardly been aware he'd been holding.

'Okay…' He hesitated. 'I need to know, are you still seeing Luke Herrington?'

'Luke—?' Her eyes went wide, and she set her cup down with a distinct clatter, spilling some of the liquid into her saucer. 'Is that why you've brought me here? To ask about my relationship with Luke Herrington? I don't see what that has to do with you.'

Jared scowled. 'It's a start.'

'Not as far as I'm concerned. It's none of your damn business.' She pushed back her chair. 'And now, if you—'

'Wait!' His hand was gripping her wrist before he could prevent himself. 'Belle, please, wait. I have to know. Can't you understand that?'

'Why?'

Jared groaned. 'Because I'm leaving Elizabeth.'

A whole gamut of emotions crossed her face at that moment, but at least she was no longer trying to leave her seat. Shock; incredulity; arrant disbelief; they were all there. And the faintest glimmer of something else he dared not let himself identify in case he was wrong. 'I don't believe you.'

Jared's thumb massaged the inner curve of her wrist. 'But you want to, don't you?'

'What kind of a question is that?' Isobel pulled her wrist out of his grasp, rubbing at the place where his thumb had been as if trying to erase any trace of his touch. 'You said you'd never leave Elizabeth. How do I know you're not just saying this now because nothing else has worked?'

Jared chose his words carefully. 'I admit, I've never attempted to gain my freedom,' he agreed. 'But that was for reasons I'd rather not go into right now. And, until I met you, I didn't care one way or the other. You have to believe me. I wouldn't lie about something like this.'

Isobel was wary. 'And what's changed your mind?'

'You have.' He gave a rueful smile. 'Is that so hard to believe? You've been driving me crazy for months.'

Isobel shook her head. 'So—have you told her?'

'Not yet—'

'I thought not.' She was visibly withdrawing from him again. 'This is just a new ploy, isn't it, Jared? You've realised that telling me how much you need me isn't going to work, so you've decided to pretend that you're going to leave Elizabeth—'

'It's not pretence,' he said harshly.

'No?'

'No.'

'So do it,' said Isobel tightly, and he could see she was trembling a little now. 'If you mean what you say, do it.'

Jared pressed a balled fist against his thigh. 'I intend to.' He stared at her with impassioned eyes. 'Will—will you come back?'

Isobel's brows drew together. 'Back?' she echoed. 'Back where?'

'Back to me, for God's sake,' he snapped grimly. 'I need to know that you still feel the same.'

Isobel expelled an unsteady breath. 'We'll see.'

'See what?' He was getting frustrated. 'See whether this man Herrington can offer you more?'

It was unforgivable, and as soon as the words were out of his mouth he knew it. But he couldn't take them back, and he watched in dismay as Isobel thrust back her chair and got to her feet.

'No,' she said with revulsion. 'No, I didn't mean that.' Her hand clutched the collar of her coat. 'And as you obviously have such a distorted opinion of me, is there any point in continuing with this charade?'

CHAPTER THIRTEEN

THERE was a car parked at Isobel's gate when she arrived home from work on Friday evening, and for a moment her heart leapt into her throat. It was a sleek grey Mercedes, and, in spite of what she'd said last Saturday, the idea that Jared had come to tell her he'd left Elizabeth sprang irresistibly into her mind.

It wasn't Jared's car. The number plate was different, she saw, as she drew closer, and unless he'd changed his car in the last few days it belonged to someone else. But who?

Despite what her common sense was telling her, she found she was trembling. Parking behind it, she couldn't dislodge Jared from her thoughts, and even the slimmest chance of seeing him again turned her bones to water.

She was a fool, she thought impatiently. Jared thought he only had to crook his little finger and she'd come running. She didn't know how he'd found out she was staying with Michelle last weekend, but after what he'd said about Luke Herrington she couldn't believe his visit had been coincidental. He'd intended to see her, to spin her his latest scheme to get her back. He'd realised that nothing less than offering to leave Elizabeth was going to produce the desired effect, but she couldn't believe he'd leave his wife—and Goldman-Lewis—just for her.

Even so, she hadn't been able to help hoping against hope that he'd meant it. On the drive back to Fenham, he'd told her he was going to speak to Elizabeth as soon as she got home. She and her father were due back on Thursday afternoon, and Jared had promised to ring Isobel on Thursday evening.

Perhaps he'd thought his words would seduce her into spending the rest of the weekend with him, she reflected now, not wanting to remember how she'd spent the whole of the previous evening waiting for his call. He hadn't rung, of course, and she'd assured herself that she'd never really expected him to, but it hadn't worked any more successfully than the dismissive account of their meeting that she'd given Michelle. Her friend had known exactly how counterfeit her attitude was, and in spite of her efforts it had soured the rest of the weekend.

That was why she'd gone to see Marion on Sunday morning. She'd dreaded telling her sister about the baby, but in the event Marion had taken it in her stride. Perhaps she wouldn't have been so understanding if Isobel had still been living in the city. But she wasn't, so she could afford to be generous.

Of course, Isobel had mentioned nothing about seeing Jared. And she was glad she hadn't now that he'd proved himself so predictably false. Besides, Marion would have had her own opinion of a man who'd promised to divorce his invalid wife because of her sister. And that might have been one mistake she couldn't forgive.

Now, however, a woman was getting out of the Mercedes. She had evidently been waiting for Isobel to get home, and she turned to give the younger woman an imperious smile.

'Mrs Dorland?' she asked, as Isobel thrust open her door and got out, and Isobel's pulse quickened. She suspected she knew who the woman was now: it was her aunt Justine.

Swallowing to hide her agitation, she went towards her. 'I'm—Isobel Dorland, yes,' she said quickly, without being any more specific.

'How do you do?' The woman was polite, but she didn't offer her hand. 'I'm Mrs Dorland, too, although I doubt if you appreciate the distinction. Can we go inside?'

Isobel was taken aback by her hostility, although she supposed she shouldn't have been. After all, Robert Dorland had taken great pains to keep her existence a secret, and she'd already decided that after the baby was born she was going to make her home somewhere else. It had been a mistake coming here, another mistake, and she'd never felt it so strongly as she did at this moment.

'Why not?' she said now, briskly, and, opening the gate, she allowed her visitor to lead the way up the path.

Justine Dorland—if that was who she was—looked much younger than Isobel's mother had done. For one thing the coil of blonde hair she wore at her nape showed no trace of grey, and the suit she was wearing revealed a trim figure. High-heeled pumps completed a picture of fashionable elegance that was only enhanced by her rather sharp features. Yet as she waited for Isobel to unlock the door there was a certain agitation in her face that was at odds with her controlled appearance.

Thankfully, the fire was still smouldering in the grate, giving the room a welcoming warmth, and Isobel bustled around, adding a couple of logs to the coals and turning on lamps. Then, when she was sure the place looked as attractive as she could make it, she turned to her visitor. 'Won't you sit down?'

The older woman hesitated and then, closing the door on the twilit afternoon, she folded her gloved hands together. 'I'd rather stand,' she declared, unconsciously tilting her head. 'This isn't a social call.'

Isobel thought about keeping her coat on to hide her thickening waistline, and then changed her mind. Dammit, she had nothing to hide from this woman, she thought crossly, only trembling a little as she slipped the jacket from her shoulders and laid it over the back of a chair.

'As you like,' she said now, keeping her hands at her sides with an effort. 'What do you want?'

'What do I want?' The woman's voice was almost shrill. 'As if you didn't know.'

Isobel quivered. 'I—don't see that my being here has anything to do with you. Not now.'

'Don't you? Don't you?' The older woman was incensed. 'I don't know how you had the nerve to come here. Setting yourself up on my doorstep as if—as if I owed you something; as if I'd care about you and your—your bastard!'

Isobel swayed a little, and grasped the back of the chair where she'd lain her coat for support. In all the thoughts she'd had since she'd found her father's letters, she'd never imagined a scene like this, and, although she could appreciate the resentment Justine felt towards her, she couldn't understand her antagonism towards her unborn child.

'If that's the way you feel, I don't know what you're doing here,' she said now, through tight lips. 'I—I haven't asked you—either of you—for anything. And nor do I intend to. As—as soon as my baby's born, I'm moving away.'

Justine looked taken aback. 'Then why did you come here?'

'I don't honestly know,' admitted Isobel wearily. 'I—needed to get away. I'd—found some letters which my father had written to my mother, and I thought—stupidly, I realise that now—that he might want to meet me.'

Justine was looking more and more confused. 'What does that have to do with your coming here? I don't care what kind of a relationship your parents had. But I have to say it sounds as if your mother's situation was not so much different from your own. Evidently you've had as little communication with your father as your child's going to have with his.'

Isobel blinked incredulously. 'You know nothing about my baby's father,' she retorted hotly.

'Oh, I think I know more than you,' replied the older woman coldly, and Isobel's lips parted.

'You—know—Jared?' she whispered, wondering if she'd made a terrible mistake. Could the woman possibly be some relation of Elizabeth's?

'Who's Jared?' the woman was asking now, and Isobel experienced a momentary pang of relief.

'Who's Jared?' she echoed. 'I thought you said you knew him.'

'I don't know anyone called Jared, and if this is some clever attempt to divert—'

'Jared's my baby's father,' broke in Isobel fiercely. 'And I don't know what the hell you're talking about.'

Now Justine—if it was Justine, and Isobel was having serious doubts—stared at her with wary eyes. 'Is that what he told you?' she whispered. 'Was that the name he used?'

Isobel couldn't take much more of this and, sinking down onto the arm of the nearby chair, she shook her head. 'That is his name,' she insisted. 'I know it's his name. I've known him and—and—well, I know his family.'

'His family?'

Justine seemed appalled, and Isobel wanted to scream with frustration. 'Yes,' she said. 'Yes. And I don't honestly know what it has to do with you.'

'I'm his wife,' cried the older woman harshly. 'And his name's not Jared. It's Robert; Robert Dorland!'

Isobel was glad she was sitting down. 'You're crazy,' she said. 'That's *my* father's name.'

'Your father!' Justine stumbled to a chair. 'You're lying!'

Isobel spread her hands. 'I'm sorry. I know it must come as quite a shock to you. I never intended to tell you like this, but you didn't give me much choice.'

Justine fumbled a tissue out of her pocket and pressed it to her lips. If anything, she looked paler than the younger woman felt at that moment, and Isobel knew a reluctant sense of sympathy for her. It must have been quite a shock to learn that her husband had a daughter older than their own children.

'Would you like some tea?' she asked, getting to her feet again, but Justine only shook her head, staring at her across the folds of the tissue as if she couldn't believe her eyes.

'Who are you?' she asked at last. 'Your name's not really Dorland, is it?'

Isobel caught her lower lip between her teeth. 'It is, actually,' she replied after a moment. 'Isobel Dorland, as I said before.'

Justine's hands dropped into her lap. 'You're *George's* daughter?' she asked faintly.

'No.' Isobel decided there was no point in lying about it now. 'I'm Robert's daughter. George and his wife adopted me twenty-six years ago.'

Justine was patently amazed. 'I had no idea.'

'Nor did I.' Isobel couldn't keep the bitterness out of her voice. 'Not until my mother—my adoptive mother—died and I found the letters he'd written to her and my father twenty-six years ago. Apparently he and—and my biological mother—met—only briefly. When she was killed soon after I was born, he arranged for the adoption.'

'My God!'

Justine was horrified, and, realising she had to say something in her father's defence, Isobel went on. 'He—he told my parents that he hadn't known anything about me until my mother died. He also said that as you couldn't have children yourself, it wouldn't be fair to—to—tell you—'

'That's—incredible!'

'I know. I—I met your daughter the other day.' Isobel grimaced. 'But of course you know that, don't you, Mrs Dorland? That's why you're here.'

Justine seemed to be trying to make some sense of what

she'd heard. Shaking her head, she said, 'I have to admit that when Barbara told me you were—well—' She broke off, clearly embarrassed now. 'I thought—oh, God, you don't want to know what I thought.'

'I do.' Isobel resumed her seat again. 'Please: I've told you a little of why I'm here. Won't you at least tell me why you came? Did—did my father send you?'

'Your father?' Justine pressed her fingers to her lips. 'Oh, dear Lord, I don't know how to tell you this, but—' She made a distressed sound. 'Robert's dead, I'm afraid. He—he died—over five months ago.'

'Five months!' Isobel caught her breath. It was almost the same length of time that she'd been pregnant. Her lips twisted. 'So I'm too late.'

'I'm afraid so.' Justine's expression was sympathetic. 'I suppose I should say I'm sorry.'

Isobel shook her head. 'It's not as if I ever knew him…'

'Nevertheless…' Justine hesitated. 'Oh, God, I came here to—well, to be frank, to get rid of you. And now I find that you have more right to expect my sympathy than any of them.'

Isobel frowned. 'Any of whom?'

'Robert's women,' said Justine flatly. 'I hate to tell you this, my dear, but your mother was not my husband's only indiscretion.'

'And you thought that I—?'

'You must forgive me.' Justine was contrite. 'I've become so bitter in recent years. I had thought that as he got older… But, no. In that particular, at least, Robert never changed.'

Isobel could only stare at her. 'You *knew* he saw other women?'

Justine nodded.

'But—' Isobel was stunned. 'Why didn't you—?'

'Leave him?' Justine shrugged now. 'I loved him. And so long as he always came back to me…'

Isobel swallowed. 'Were there any other—any other children?'

'Not that I know of.' Justine gazed into space. 'There have been other claims over the years, of course. That's why I was so incensed to think that you—' She broke off, raising an apologetic hand. 'You see, the Dorlands used to be a wealthy family, and there were always women willing to allege that Robert had seduced them, and that the child they were carrying—' She broke off again, evidently overcome with emotion. Then, after regaining her composure, she continued unsteadily, 'Robert always denied their claims, and I suppose I always wanted to believe he wouldn't lie to me. His womanising—I could stand that. But I always insisted that if I ever found out he'd given some other woman the child I couldn't have...'

'But you have children,' protested Isobel, aware that she was feeling sorry for this woman. The more she learned about the man who had been her father, the less regret she felt at never having known him. But Justine...

'Our children are adopted,' confessed Justine after a moment, and Isobel knew a brief spurt of shame at the relief she felt at learning that at least some of what he'd told her parents was true. 'Barbara and Will are twins we adopted when they were six months old.' She paused, and then added with great dignity, 'I was born without a uterus. I was never able to give Robert the children which I think he so badly wanted.'

Isobel sat for some time after Justine had gone, mulling over the things the other woman had told her. Now that the need to maintain her composure was no longer necessary, she couldn't prevent the tears from streaming down her cheeks, though whether she was crying for her father or herself, she wasn't absolutely sure.

Oddly enough, there was a certain sense of relief in knowing that the decision about whether to contact her

father or not had been taken out of her hands. She was
sorry he was dead, even though he had played such a
superficial role in her life, but the misgivings she'd had
since coming here now all seemed justified and she desperately wanted to get away.

For her part, Justine had been amazingly understanding.
Bearing in mind the fact that she'd been so opposed to her
husband siring a child in his lifetime, she'd shown Isobel
great respect. It was as if she'd recognised something of
her husband in his daughter and, now that Robert was
gone, she was prepared to sustain his memory in any way
she could. Whether her own son and daughter would share
their mother's feelings was another matter, and Isobel was
not sufficiently sure of her own identity to want to find
out.

Justine had explained so many things. Not least the reason why George Dorland had abandoned the family home.
Apparently his father had been a womaniser, too, like his
second son, and George had been disgusted when, only
six weeks after their mother had died, John Dorland had
brought one of the village women to live at Tregarth Hall.

In those days, the Dorlands had been the wealthiest
landowners in the district, but times had changed. Farms
had had to be sold to sustain an increasingly obsolete way
of life, and by the time of John Dorland's death the estate
had shrunk alarmingly. These days, Will ran things himself, and had done so since before his father's death, while
Barbara had been in the United States for the past three
months, learning advanced farming methods at a college
in the mid-west.

Justine had also speculated about how Robert had found
it so easy to deceive her.

She'd explained that after the rift that George's departure had created between the brothers they had never been
friends, and it must have been a simple matter after their
father died to allow whatever connection there had been

to lapse completely. Until Justine had had reason to doubt her husband's word, she'd been more than willing to accept Robert's version of events, and by the time she'd suspected that George might have had some justification for his behaviour, it had been far too late to attempt to heal the breach.

Isobel had to accept that she'd never know what, if anything, her father had felt towards her mother. From what she'd learned, it would seem that Robert hadn't been capable of sustaining a relationship with any woman, even his wife, and she reflected that she'd been lucky to have been brought up by people who'd really cared about her.

She was glad now that she'd known none of this until after her adopted parents were dead. George Dorland had been right to keep it from her, for there was no doubt it would have hurt him terribly if she'd insisted on meeting her real father. Hurt her, too, she acknowledged, aware that Justine Dorland would not have been half as sympathetic if her husband had still been alive. And the man Isobel had sought had never existed—except in her imagination. He'd handed her over to his old housekeeper— Justine had told her that a Mrs Mattless, 'Matty', had worked at the Hall years ago—and that was the last he'd seen of her.

During the next couple of days, Isobel came to terms with the fact that until the baby was born she would have to stay where she was. She had nowhere else to go, after all, and, much as she wanted to escape, she had responsibilities both to herself and to her unborn child.

Justine rang once, suggesting that she might like to visit Tregarth Hall, but Isobel didn't feel as if she wanted to get involved with her father's family. It wasn't as if Justine's children were her brother and sister, and, much as she appreciated the effort Justine was making, she didn't think she and the other woman could ever be friends.

CHAPTER FOURTEEN

JARED stood at the window, staring out at the lights that were slowly appearing in the wing opposite. It wasn't yet five o'clock, but the afternoon had been dull and overcast, and the twinkling lights gave a superficial warmth to the stark bulk of the hospital buildings.

Within the private ward where he was standing there was warmth, too, but precious little comfort. The man in the iron-railed bed was still alive, but only just, his vital organs monitored by the bank of machines to which he was attached by a clutch of tubes and cables.

However, at this moment, Jared's thoughts were not on the unconscious man behind him. He was thinking about Isobel; about the effect Howard's illness would have on their relationship—if they still had a relationship, he reflected grimly—and how difficult it was going to be for him to ask Elizabeth for a divorce now.

God, was it only a little over a week since he'd seen Isobel? It seemed like a lifetime, the events that had come between then and now responsible for his present state of despair.

He'd promised to ring her Thursday night, to tell her that he'd spoken to Elizabeth, and that, no matter what obstacles she and her father might put in his path, he had taken the first steps towards gaining his freedom.

But he hadn't rung. How could he have? On Thursday night he'd been at the hospital all night, keeping vigil with Elizabeth while her father had had the first of the two operations he'd had since he'd been flown home from Greece.

Jared groaned, and raked long fingers through his hair,

allowing his hands to rest frustratedly at the back of his neck. When the phone had rung on Wednesday evening, he'd practically flung himself across the room to answer it. He'd had some crazy notion that it might be Isobel, that, knowing Elizabeth was still away, she'd taken the chance of calling him at home.

Why she would do such a thing when she'd made it plain that she was only prepared to judge him by his deeds, not his words, he didn't know. But hope sprang eternal, and it had only been when he'd heard his wife's hysterical voice that he'd been forced to abandon such foolishness.

The line had been bad. She had apparently been calling from the ship, and the reception had been distorted and intermittent. But the panic she had communicated to him had been unmistakable. Her father had had a heart attack, she'd said. He'd collapsed after dinner that evening, and he needed immediate treatment.

Jared's reactions had been automatic. After ascertaining that the cruise ship was returning to Mandraki, one of the smaller Greek islands and its nearest port-of-call, Jared had said he would make arrangements for an air ambulance to fly out and rendezvous with the ship there. Howard could be flown back to England at once, and Elizabeth should be ready to accompany him home.

Since then, none of them had had the opportunity for a prolonged conversation. Howard's condition had been critical, and Jared had wondered if the old man would make it. He'd also wondered what had happened to cause the attack, and he couldn't help the unwilling thought that perhaps Elizabeth had at last come clean about what she'd done.

Whatever, in recent days he'd been too concerned about the old man's health to tackle her about it. Besides, Elizabeth had seemed uncharacteristically vulnerable since her return. Even Janet, who had flown home separately with all the luggage, had been doing her best not to get in anyone's way.

It had obviously been a traumatic experience for both women, and Jared could sympathise with their feelings. It must have been frightening to find the old man in that state on a ship with only minimal medical facilities. Particularly as Elizabeth had always relied on her father so much.

So the promise Jared had made to Isobel had had to be put on hold. He intended to ring her, as soon as he had some positive news to give her, but with each day that passed, he grew more and more fearful that she might never want to speak to him again.

Jared heaved a weary sigh, half turning to look back at the man in the bed. Howard was peaceful now, but until the blocked valve that had caused his collapse had been cleared, it had been touch and go. When he'd first arrived at the hospital in Newcastle, he'd been too weak to stand major surgery, and the specialist who had taken charge of his case had explained that for the present they were only able to perform a stabilising operation.

Now, however, with the blockage removed, the prognosis was far more optimistic, and to Jared's amazement there was already talk of getting Howard out of bed and moving around again. It had apparently been proved that heart patients responded well to gentle stimulation, and Jared was looking forward to seeing the old man sitting up and taking notice.

A sound alerted him to the fact that there was some movement in the bed, and, leaving his position by the window, Jared went to the old man's side. Howard was stirring, and although Jared knew he should call the nurse on duty, he took a moment to reassure himself that he was not mistaken.

Howard looked so old, he thought, the hand lying limply on the coverlet so pale and ridged with veins. He'd aged enormously in the last few days, and Jared wished there was something he could do to ease his pain.

'Am I going to live?'

The whispered question caught Jared unawares, and, catching a breath, he dropped to a crouch beside the bed. 'What kind of a question is that?' he demanded, his voice gruff with emotion. 'Of course you are.' He covered the old man's hand with his own for a moment and then straightened. 'I'll get the nurse—'

'No—wait.' Howard's voice was weak, but determined. 'Not yet, Jared.'

Jared frowned, but, not wanting to upset him, he stayed where he was. 'How do you feel?'

'Sore,' admitted Howard ruefully. He frowned. 'Where am I?'

'Don't you remember?' Jared pulled a chair across to the bed and straddled it. 'You collapsed on board the cruise ship and—'

'I know that.' Howard was impatient and Jared remembered that the doctor who'd flown out with the air ambulance had told him that the old man had been drifting in and out of consciousness on the flight home. 'I meant— what hospital is this?'

'The County,' said Jared at once. 'They flew you into Newcastle airport.'

'Ah.' Howard seemed relieved. 'And you meant it? I am going to make it? That's the truth?'

Jared's smile was ironic. 'So they say. You just gave us all one hell of a scare, that's all.'

Howard's expression darkened. 'Liza most of all, I'll bet,' he muttered grimly. 'Dammit, Jared, why didn't you tell me?'

'Tell you?' Jared was confused. 'Tell you what?'

'About her and—and that woman, of course,' exclaimed Howard harshly. 'If I'd had some warning, it wouldn't have been such a—such a God-awful shock when I walked in there and found them together.'

'Wait a minute.' Jared was missing something here, and although he suspected that the last thing he should be doing at this moment was encouraging Howard to expend what little strength he had, he had to know what he meant. 'I don't know what the hell you're talking about.'

'It's no use, Jared.' Howard's blue eyes were wet with tears. 'You don't need to try and protect me any more. This is why you and Liza never had any children, isn't it? Why you took up with that Dorland woman whose car ran into yours all those months ago?'

Jared stared at him. 'You knew about that?'

'Not initially.' Howard expelled a weary breath. 'But when it became obvious that you and Elizabeth weren't trying to patch up your differences, I made a few enquiries of my own.'

'But it wasn't like that,' said Jared, feeling the need to set the record straight at last, but Howard wasn't really listening to him. He was too wrapped up with what he was trying to say.

'I should have realised what was going on sooner.' Howard groaned. 'I knew you weren't the kind of man to cheat on his wife without a reason. You've always been a decent man. Dammit, you even took the blame for the accident when you could have turned me down.'

'Howard—'

'No, hear me out.' The old man seemed determined to bare his soul, and there was no stopping him. 'I want you to know what a pathetic fool I've been.' He panted a little, but his determination was resolute. 'No wonder you found it so difficult to tell me the truth.'

'What truth?' asked Jared helplessly, but Howard just went on.

'I—I went to her cabin to talk to her,' he continued doggedly. 'She'd seemed so relaxed while we were away, and I thought it was the ideal opportunity to discuss what Beaumont had said.'

His breath caught then, and for a moment Jared was afraid he'd gone too far. But then, after drawing a laboured gulp of air, he added, 'They were there, both of them; Liza and that—that awful Brady woman—in bed—together—'

'Mr Kendall!'

The nurse's disapproving tones prevented any response Jared might have made, even if he could have found the words. Somehow he managed to push himself away from the chair and get to his feet. But his brain felt numb, and there was no co-ordination in his movements.

'I asked you to inform me immediately if the patient regained consciousness, Mr Kendall,' the nurse declared sharply. 'Mr Goldman is still a very sick man, and you had no right to engage him in conversation.'

Jared shook his head. 'I'm sorry,' he muttered, too dazed by what he'd learned to marshal a competent defence.

Ignoring the woman's censure, Howard spoke again. 'Blame me,' he wheezed, reaching for his son-in-law's hand and giving it a weak squeeze. 'We'll talk later. Right?'

Jared nodded, and although he was sure the nurse was regarding him a little strangely now, somehow he got himself out of the room.

But, in the corridor, he stood for several minutes, trying to come to terms with what Howard had told him. Was it true? Were Elizabeth and Janet Brady lovers? God, the idea was unbelievable, and yet it explained so much. Made sense of so many things. Not least Elizabeth's reasons for marrying him...

He found his way almost automatically to the visitors' lounge, where he'd spent so many hours in recent days, and was brought up short at the sight of his wife and Janet Brady sharing a tray of tea that one of the orderlies must have provided for them. Apart from the two women, the lounge was deserted, and he paused in the doorway, both hands braced on the lintel, waiting for them to notice him.

They were huddled over the table, he saw, and Jared felt an almost overwhelming sense of outrage at what their intimacy had achieved. How could he have failed to recognise what must have been going on for so long? he wondered bitterly. How long had Elizabeth intended to keep her sexuality a secret? Until her father was dead?

Well, she'd almost succeeded...

As if sensing the hostility he was projecting, his wife looked up at that moment and saw him. Immediately, she withdrew the hand that Janet had been holding, and, swinging her wheelchair round, came towards him with anxious eyes.

'What is it? What's wrong?' she exclaimed. 'Is it Daddy? Has he had a relapse?'

Jared lifted an indifferent shoulder. 'Do you really care?' he asked coldly.

'Of course I care.' Elizabeth searched his face with a troubled gaze. 'He's my father.'

'So he is.' Jared managed to contain his anger with an effort. 'Thank you for reminding me.'

Elizabeth gasped. 'Why are you being like this, Jared? You know I've been worried out of my mind. If Daddy is worse, for God's sake, tell me. I've just been reassuring Janet that the operation was a success.'

Jared's lips curled. 'And I'm sure Janet was pleased to hear that.'

'She was.' Elizabeth cast a nervous glance back at the other woman. 'She's very fond of Daddy, as you know.'

'Do I?' Jared's arms fell to his sides and, as if fearing he was about to touch her, Elizabeth drew back. But her husband only gave a sardonic smile at this evidence of her alarm. 'I don't know anything, do I? Don't they say it's always the husband who's the last to hear?'

'I think that's the wife,' said Elizabeth curtly, and then, as if realising what he'd said, her eyes went wide. 'I—' She swallowed hard. 'Is Daddy awake?'

'Only just,' replied Jared. And then, because he couldn't stand her pathetic attempt to normalise the situation, 'You could have killed him! Do you realise that?'

Elizabeth's lips quivered. 'He's told you, hasn't he?'

'Did you think he wouldn't?'

'I—I hoped—'

'Oh, yes?' Jared's hands balled into fists. 'I just bet you did.'

'No, you don't understand.' Elizabeth glanced over her shoulder again. 'I—hoped I'd have a chance to tell you myself.'

Jared's disbelief was obvious. 'So why didn't you?'

'Oh, God, I don't know.' Elizabeth groaned now. 'There—there just hasn't been time—'

'In four years!' Jared was contemptuous. 'Forgive me, but I don't believe you.'

'Well—what with the accident and everything—'

Jared's lips tightened. 'You had to bring that up, didn't you?'

'Well, why not?' Elizabeth sensed a weakness and went straight for it. 'I could say I didn't have any kind of a life until the accident, but I won't give you that satisfaction. All the same, I'm not sorry it happened. Do you hear me? If I hadn't crashed the car, Janet and I might never have met.'

Jared blinked. Had Elizabeth said what he thought she'd said? That *she'd* crashed the car?

But before he could find his voice to challenge her words, she went on, 'In any case, we can't talk about it now. I want to see Daddy—'

'Wait!' Jared deliberately blocked the doorway, determined to find a way to get her to repeat herself. 'Are you saying you—you were unhappy before the crash?'

Elizabeth gave him a scornful look. 'What do you think? Don't pretend you didn't know how I was feeling. You were going to leave me; I know you were.' She lowered her voice. 'After—after the abortion, you could hardly bear to look at me.'

Jared's voice was harsh. 'Do you blame me?'

'No.' For once, Elizabeth was being honest. 'But you couldn't expect me to be glad about it. Daddy would never have forgiven me if he'd found out. That was why—'

She broke off abruptly, but Jared couldn't let her stop there. He had a horrible inkling that he knew what was coming next, but he had to hear it from her lips. 'What?' he demanded, taking an involuntary step towards her. 'What?'

'Why I wished I'd killed us both, of course,' muttered Elizabeth in a tortured voice. She pressed the heels of her hands to her eyes. 'Now—now can I go and see Daddy?'

CHAPTER FIFTEEN

ISOBEL stood at the door, waving, until Michelle's car was out of sight. Then, quelling the urge to burst into tears, she turned and went back into the cottage.

The coffee cups they'd used after lunch were still on the table, and, gathering them up, Isobel carried them into the kitchen. She ran water into the bowl and added a liquid cleanser, then, plunging her hands into the suds, she started to wash up.

It had been good of her friend to come, she assured herself fiercely. It was a long way for anyone to drive, particularly as it was only two weeks since Isobel had spent that awkward weekend in Newcastle. Even thinking that Michelle had got a certain amount of satisfaction out of telling her about Howard Goldman's heart attack was pathetic. Of course her friend had taken some pride in having her feelings justified. She'd warned Isobel to be wary of Jared from the start.

Nevertheless, she wasn't altogether sorry that Michelle had gone. Keeping up a brave face over the last couple of days had drained her emotional resources completely, especially since at the beginning of the weekend she'd misunderstood Michelle's reasons for telling her what she had.

She was such a fool, she thought now, feeling the hot tears stinging her eyes. She'd thought at first that the news of Howard Goldman's illness meant that Jared had a legitimate excuse for not getting in touch with her, as he'd promised. But, according to Michelle, it was ten days since Howard had been flown home from his holiday, and it was rumoured that although he was making a good recovery, he was not expected to return to the office.

165

Which meant, Michelle had remarked slyly, that Jared
had taken over the running of Goldman-Lewis in his absence. 'It's an ill wind, as they say,' she'd observed drily,
and Isobel had realised at that moment that what Michelle
was really saying was that there was no chance of Jared
asking Elizabeth for a divorce now.

Finishing the dishes, Isobel dried her hands on a towel
and returned to the living room. But the firelit warmth of
the room offered no comfort at present, and, collecting her
jacket from the hall, she let herself out of the front door.

It was a cold afternoon, but it was fine, and a watery
sun was doing its best to give beauty to the stark silhou-
ettes of the trees on the green. As she walked along, she
tried to put all thoughts of Jared and his promises out of
her mind, but it was impossible now to ignore the truth
behind Michelle's words. He could have phoned her; he
should have phoned her—if only to tell her what had happened—but it was two weeks now, and there'd been no
communication whatsoever.

She should have expected it, she thought bitterly. After
all, it was a classic case of two people, each wanting different things from a relationship. He wasn't to blame; she
was. She'd always known that Elizabeth had an unbreak-
able hold on his loyalties, and despite what Michelle had
said she knew he didn't take his responsibilities lightly.

There was a copse of trees at the end of the village and,
although she would have liked to have gone further, she
turned back. Twilight was approaching and she wasn't
reckless enough to tackle lonely country lanes on her own,
especially not after dark. Besides, she had no wish to encounter anyone she knew either. She'd done rather well
so far, but she knew Tregarth Hall was in that direction,
too, and that was an added deterrent.

The big car coming towards her in the fading light
looked suspiciously like Justine Dorland's car, however,
and, hoping she wouldn't be recognised, Isobel drew back

into the shadows cast by the surrounding trees. The car slowed, and Isobel thought it was just her luck to be found here. Whatever she said, Justine was bound to think she'd had some ulterior motive for spying out the land around the Hall. She'd never believe that Isobel's thoughts had been far from Polgarron, or that talking to her new-found relatives was the last thing she wanted to do.

The car stopped, and for a few moments nothing happened. Then, realising it was up to her to make a brave face of it, Isobel plastered a smile on her lips and turned towards the vehicle. She had as much right to be here as anyone else, she told herself impatiently, and then was taken aback when the passenger door was shoved open from inside, and a harsh voice said, 'Get in.'

It was Jared's voice, and Isobel's lips parted incredulously. She'd been so sure it was Justine's car and she stared at the dark blur of his face in shocked disbelief.

'I said, get in,' he repeated, his tone sharpening almost aggressively, and Isobel caught her breath as another thought occurred to her.

Despite the lateness of the afternoon, he had evidently been able to recognise her at once, and the realisation that he must have seen her quite clearly in his headlights caused her to draw the sides of her jacket closer about her. But it was too late. She knew it. The sheepskin jacket couldn't disguise the rounded curve of her belly as the cashmere coat she'd worn in Newcastle had done, and she shivered at the anticipation of his reaction.

'What—what are you doing here?' she asked then, making no attempt to do as he'd asked, and with a muffled oath he thrust open his door and got out.

'Get in and I'll tell you,' he said, making no attempt to hide the fact that he was staring at her stomach. 'I think we have a lot to talk about, don't you?'

Isobel couldn't help it: her hand went almost automatically to the mound that pushed the sides of her jacket

apart, and, as if he didn't trust himself, Jared swung open
his door and got back into the Mercedes.

The passenger door was still ajar, and, realising she was
only putting off the inevitable, Isobel moved almost me-
chanically towards the car. Without saying anything else
she got in beside him, and Jared didn't speak to her as he
reversed into the gateway where she had been standing
and turned the car around.

'How—how did you know where I was?' she asked as
he drove through the village, feeling obliged to make some
attempt to normalise the situation. But all he did was turn
to give her a brooding look, and she fell silent again.

They reached the cottage in record time, and this time
Jared didn't hesitate before getting out of the car. Isobel
had barely had time to open her door before he was swinging it wide for her, waiting with taciturn stillness for her
to alight. He offered his hand, but she didn't take it, pre-
ferring instead to use the frame of the door to help her to
get to her feet, and his features tightened at this obvious
display of pride.

'Are—are you coming in?' she asked, knowing it would
annoy him, but needing to assert her independence, and
Jared slammed her door behind her.

'Try and stop me,' he replied, with harsh intensity, and
her knees felt decidedly shaky as she hastened up the path.

She found her key but she had some difficulty getting
it into the lock, and, despite her resistance, he took it from
her. He had no problem in opening the door, and she made
no attempt to hide her resentment at his high-handed behaviour.

'I'm not a child, you know,' she said tightly, only hes-
itating a moment before taking off her jacket. She held up
her head. 'Why are you looking at me like that?'

'For God's sake, Belle!' He had closed the door and
was now standing staring at her with tortured eyes. 'Don't

expect me to behave as if I'm not in a state of shock. Why the hell didn't you tell me?'

Isobel trembled. She couldn't help it. Seeing him again had been traumatic enough without having to face his anger as well. 'You know why,' she answered unsteadily. 'You—you're married. You'll never leave Elizabeth, I know that.' She swallowed. 'Especially now.'

Jared shook his head. 'Is that what your friend told you?' he demanded. 'I should have known she hadn't come here to sing my praises.'

'Michelle?' Isobel's brows drew together. 'You know Michelle's been here?'

'I should do,' he said harshly, stepping away from the door. 'I've been waiting for her to leave for the past twenty-four hours.'

Isobel caught her breath. 'You've been here in the village for twenty-four hours?'

'No.' Jared's lips twisted. 'I've been staying at a hotel in Polgarth, but I've driven by here a dozen times in the past two days.'

'So why didn't you—?'

'What?' He halted in front of her and she was intensely conscious of the curve of her belly swelling between them. 'Come in?' And, at her involuntary nod, 'I wanted to see you alone. I had things to say to you. After the last occasion I tried to speak to you when she was there, I preferred to wait.' His eyes dropped significantly. 'I didn't think then that a day more or less would make any difference, and I guessed she'd be going back today.'

Isobel was terribly self-conscious. It was the first time he'd seen her like this and she couldn't help thinking that he was probably remembering the slim, moderately attractive young woman he had had an affair with. She looked nothing like that now. In black leggings and the chunky cream sweater that used to be his, she was anything but attractive, and she wished she'd had some warning of this meeting.

He, on the other hand, looked much the same as ever. His lean muscled frame had always looked good in jeans and tee shirts, and his black suede jerkin accentuated his raw masculinity. She could see why she'd fallen in love with him, why she'd always love him, and she wondered if Elizabeth had any idea how lucky she was.

'May I touch?' he asked suddenly, and Isobel was instantly aware of the intimacy of the situation. His words were disturbing and unexpected, and, as if reacting to her mood, the baby chose that moment to make its presence felt.

He must have seen it, because instead of waiting for her permission his hands spread possessively over her stomach. 'I can feel it,' he said, his eyes lifting to hers in sudden amazement, and she wondered if it was only pride in his offspring's exertions that gave his expression such bone-melting warmth.

'He—she—is very active,' said Isobel awkwardly, feeling the heat of his hands penetrating the layers of clothing that separated her skin from his. She would have drawn back then, but he wouldn't let her, and in an effort to regain some sense of her own identity, she added, 'I—I was sorry to hear about Mr Goldman. It must have been a terrible shock for—for all of you.'

'Howard's going to be okay,' said Jared almost absently, his hands still shaping the curve of her abdomen. Then, with a groan of impatience, his hands moved to her hips and he pulled her against him. 'I've missed you so much,' he muttered roughly. 'I was so afraid you wouldn't want to see me again.'

Isobel swallowed. 'What makes you think I do?' she protested, trying not to respond to the provocative pressure of his thighs. 'Michelle says you've taken over the running of Goldman-Lewis. Is that true?'

Jared closed his eyes for a moment and then, cupping her face in his hands, he said roughly, 'Whatever happens at Goldman-Lewis is nothing to do with why I'm here.'

'Isn't it?' Isobel gained strength from the fact that he hadn't given her a straight answer. 'Please don't insult my intelligence by pretending that you have any intention of leaving Elizabeth now.'

Jared stared at her, and then, taking a step back, he pulled off his glasses and massaged the cleft that had formed between his brows with his thumb and forefinger 'That's some opinion you've got of me, isn't it?' he remarked bitterly. 'Do you honestly think I'd put my position at Goldman-Lewis before us?'

'I don't know, do I?' Isobel was determined not to be diverted by his apparent vulnerability. 'Have you told Elizabeth you want a divorce?'

Jared uttered a harsh laugh. 'Oh, yes. She knows.'

'She does?' Isobel was taken aback. 'But—'

'Yes, *but*,' muttered Jared, returning his glasses to his nose and raking his hands through his hair. 'When you hear what I have to say, you may still want to send me away.'

'What are you talking about?' Isobel stared at him.

Jared shook his head. 'I don't know where to begin.' Then, glancing towards the fire, he added wearily, 'Do you mind if we sit down?'

'I—of course.'

Isobel gestured automatically towards the sofa, but although he only took up half the couch, she chose to perch on the edge of the armchair opposite.

Jared noticed, but although his expression mirrored his feelings, he didn't offer any protest. Instead, he spent the next few moments staring into the fire before saying flatly, 'Elizabeth has been having an affair. With Janet Brady.'

Isobel's jaw dropped. 'With Janet Brady?'

'Yeah.' Jared's shoulders sagged. 'Ironic, isn't it? I never suspected a thing.'

'But how did you...? When did you...?' Isobel broke off, and then added helplessly, 'Does her father know?'

'He does now,' said Jared pointedly, and Isobel caught her breath.

'Are you saying it had something to do with his heart attack?' She was appalled. 'I can hardly believe it.'

'It's true.' Jared sounded exhausted. 'He told me so himself.'

Isobel shook her head. 'So how do you feel?'

'How do I feel?' Jared shrugged. 'I don't feel anything for her except indifference. My feelings all depend on you.'

'On me?' Isobel stared at him.

'On whether you're prepared to take me back,' said Jared, leaning forward, his forearms resting on his thighs. 'I had hopes when we talked a couple of weeks ago, but since then—hell, I don't take anything for granted any more.'

Isobel hesitated. 'Do you want me back?'

He scowled. 'What kind of a question is that?'

'A perfectly reasonable one, I'd have thought,' she replied carefully. 'When you came here, you didn't know about—about this.' Her hand sought her abdomen again.

Jared blew out a breath. 'And you think that might make a difference?'

'Well—' She paused. 'It may be a silly remark in the circumstances, but you and Elizabeth didn't have any children, did you? Was that her choice or yours?'

Jared hesitated. 'We did have a child,' he said at last, heavily. 'Or, at least, we were going to. Elizabeth had an abortion three years ago. I knew nothing about it until it was over. Needless to say, if I'd known...'

'Oh, Jared!'

He bent his head. 'I told you we'd been having problems before—before the accident...'

'That was what you meant?' Isobel pressed her fingers to her lips. 'But then, of course, there was the crash, and after that I suppose you felt compelled to stay with her. Oh, Jared, it must have been terrible—'

'No.' Jared broke in then. 'Well, yes, the accident was terrible, and I did stay with her. But—I wasn't driving when we had the crash.'

'But everyone said you were—'

'It was what Howard wanted,' explained Jared flatly. 'I know it sounds crazy now, but at the time it seemed like such a little thing—'

'A little thing!' Isobel was aghast. 'You took the blame for crippling your wife!'

'No one knew she was going to be permanently paralysed by the crash. Elizabeth had been drinking. I hadn't. It wasn't until it was too late to do anything about it that I found out she'd never walk again.'

Isobel didn't know what to say. 'Didn't you—didn't you resent it?' she asked at last, and he gave her a wry look.

'Often,' he agreed. 'But Elizabeth suffered much more than I did, at least in the beginning, and our relationship— hers and mine, that is—had soured me for anyone else. Until I met you.' He sighed. 'I wanted to tell you. But until recently she'd always maintained that she didn't remember that evening at all.'

'And she did?' Isobel was struggling to understand, but it wasn't easy. She had the feeling it would take longer than a few minutes to take it all in. 'So why didn't you ring?' she protested at last, desperate to regain some semblance of normality, and with a groan of anguish Jared dropped onto his knees at her feet.

'Because I wanted to see you,' he said huskily. 'Because I wanted to tell you myself what had happened.' His hands curved over her thighs as he looked at her. 'Because I didn't know how you'd react when I told you about Elizabeth. Unfortunately someone else beat me to it.'

Isobel trembled. 'Michelle means well.'

'I'll take your word for it,' said Jared drily. Then, bending to rest his cheek against her stomach, he added thickly, 'God, Belle, how long do I have to wait? Do you forgive me? Do you want me?' He moaned softly. 'Because, God forgive me, I don't think I can live without you.'

Isobel's hands came up, almost of their own accord, and lifted his face to hers. 'We—we come as a package deal,' she murmured softly, and, taking off his glasses, she leant towards him and kissed each cheek in turn. 'Are you sure you want us both?'

'I'm sure,' said Jared fiercely, leaning over her and pressing a tender kiss to the corner of her mouth. 'You're the only woman I've ever loved.'

'Me?' Her voice was husky with emotion. 'Oh, God, Jared, you have no idea how much I've wanted to hear you say that—to see you—to share this—' She drew his hands to her stomach again. 'To share our baby with you.'

'Don't bet on it.' Jared's voice was rough. 'If I'd only known. You almost had me convinced that you didn't need me any more.'

Isobel made a rueful sound. 'I've always needed you,' she admitted unsteadily. 'But I was never sure what you wanted.'

'What I wanted?' Jared eyes sought hers in arrant disbelief. 'But surely you knew how I felt about you?'

'I thought I did.'

Jared frowned. 'What does that mean?'

'That evening—at the hotel in Polgarth—you told me you didn't know what love was.'

'Oh, God!' Jared's cool fingers caressed her jaw now. 'I was jealous that evening. I'd found you with another man, and I guess I wanted to hurt you as much as you were hurting me. I lashed out. I shouldn't have, but when you told me you never wanted to see me again, I hated myself for the mess I'd made of my life.'

'Do you mean that?'

'I mean it,' he assured her huskily. His thumb found

the corner of her mouth and traced the shape of her lips with aching tenderness. 'I'm not making excuses, but until you came along there hadn't been much affection in my life. When I was a kid, I'd been slung from one children's home to another, never knowing if the next place was going to be any better than the last. Then, later, when I realised Elizabeth had only married me to get her father off her back, I began to believe that life was only about using people. Even the accident, and its aftermath, only reinforced my opinion that there was no such thing as selfless love.' He shook his head. 'Then I met you.' His eyes darkened. 'And I treated you in exactly the same way as everyone else had treated me. I didn't want to believe that there might be something more than a sexual attraction between us. That would have meant me revising my opinion of everything I believed in and it wasn't until you went away that I realised what I'd lost.'

'Oh, Jared...' There were tears trembling on Isobel's lids now, and she grasped his hands and brought them clumsily to her lips. 'I've missed you so much. If it hadn't been for—for this, I'd probably have given in and come back to you. But I kept telling myself that I'd have your baby, and that was what kept me going.'

'Belle...' Jared got to his feet and drew her up with him. He pulled her into his arms, the mound of her belly cradled between them. 'I love you, I need you; I want you; and I never want us to be apart again.'

He kissed her then, his lips slanting tenderly across her mouth, his hands moving from her hips to the small of her back. But his touch was gentle, undemanding, as if he was afraid he might hurt the baby, and it was Isobel who had to solicit a more satisfying embrace. 'Kiss me properly,' she protested, arching her body against him until she could feel the reassuring thrust of his maleness. 'Open your mouth.'

Her tongue pressed eagerly between his lips, and although she felt his momentary withdrawal, the need he'd been stifling for so long was stronger than he knew. 'Belle...' he groaned, in a final bid for sanity, but Isobel wouldn't let him go.

'I'm not made of sugar,' she breathed, circling his ear with her tongue. 'I won't melt.'

'But—'

'But, nothing.' She looked into his eyes, her own moist with emotion. 'Don't you want to make love with me?'

'Ah, God—'

That was a question he could only answer in one way, and, giving in to his own eager longings, he covered her mouth with his again.

Now it was his tongue that surged deeply into the dark cavern of her mouth, taking possession of its yielding sweetness in the way that mimicked what he wanted to do with her body. His hands cupped her bottom, lifting her against him, and, despite the pressure of her belly, his manhood was wedged against the feminine softness of her mound.

'Do you have any idea how long I've waited to do this?' he asked, his voice muffled in the soft curve of her neck. 'Sometimes I think that was all that kept me sane. The hope that at some time in the future we'd be together again.' He drew an unsteady breath. 'And now we are.'

'Not quite,' said Isobel huskily, stepping back and taking his hand. 'Let's go upstairs.'

'Upstairs?' Jared blinked. 'Um—where are my glasses?' They'd fallen earlier, and now he started looking all around for them. 'They must be here somewhere—'

'Jared!' She gazed anxiously at him. 'Does the way I look put you off?'

'Don't be crazy!' Jared's response was harsh, but he continued to look about him. 'Where the hell are they?'

'You won't need them where we're going,' she told him firmly. 'Will you?'

Jared raked back his hair with an unsteady hand. 'Are you sure—I mean, is this wise?'

Isobel sighed. 'Is what wise?'

'Us.' A faint colour stained his cheeks. 'You.' He groaned. 'You know what I mean.'

Isobel's lips tilted. 'I don't care if it's wise or not,' she told him simply. 'I can't wait.' She paused. 'Can you?'

Jared's response was to bend and scoop her up into his arms. 'Let's say, you've just persuaded me,' he murmured, inhaling her distinctive fragrance with evident satisfaction. He nodded towards the door into the hall. 'I guess it's this way…'

Isobel's bedroom had never seemed smaller than when Jared set her on her feet and stood looking about him. His tall muscled body dwarfed the modest contours of the room, his darkness throwing the white eyelet bedspread into sharp relief.

'Do you like it?' asked Isobel softly, the confidence that had filled her downstairs dissipating with the proximity of taking off her clothes in front of him. It wasn't that she hadn't done it before, but the memory of the reflection she'd seen in her mirror that morning kept her from behaving naturally.

'I like who's in it more,' responded Jared, tossing his jacket aside and loosening the belt of his jeans. Then, noticing that she wasn't following his example, he unfastened the button at his waist but didn't go any further. 'What's wrong?'

'Nothing.'

Isobel shook her head, staring greedily at the glimpse of his stomach she could see below the hem of his tee shirt. A triangle of hair-covered skin was visible where his zip had slid partway down, impelled by the powerful swell of his erection, and she ached to go to him and slip her hand inside his jeans.

'Belle!' He could see her staring at him, and his voice was rough with feeling. 'Come here.'

Isobel trembled. 'I can't.'

'Why not?'

Her hands curved over her stomach. 'I've changed, Jared—'

'I can see that.' There was humour in his voice at first, but then, seeing her distress, he sobered. 'You look—beautiful.'

'I look ugly,' she contradicted him, looking down, and with a muffled exclamation he covered the space between them.

'Is that what this is all about?' he demanded, grasping her chin and tipping her face up to his. 'Don't you want me to see you?'

She shook her head. 'I look—grotesque.'

'I don't agree.' Taking control, he peeled the cream sweater over her head, and then smiled at the full breasts that now swelled over her lacy bra. 'You're beautiful. You'll always be beautiful to me.'

He slid the leggings over her hips and then pressed her down onto the bed so that he could pull them down her legs. When she was naked except for her bra and panties, he surveyed her with intense satisfaction. 'Beautiful, as I said.'

'Oh, Jared!' Leaning forward, she put her arms around his neck, and bestowed a kiss on his neck. 'I do love you.'

'I should hope so,' he teased her gently, releasing himself briefly to step out of his trousers and pull his tee shirt over his head. Then he joined her on the bed. 'I don't intend to let you go again.'

Her underwear was soon disposed of and then, with infinite tenderness, he bent to kiss her breasts. He suckled from each swollen nipple in turn, teasing them with his tongue and tugging on the sensitive flesh. At the same time his hands shaped the burgeoning swell of her stomach, before dipping to cup the dark curls at the apex of her legs.

Isobel arched against his hand, and his fingers slipped between the petals to find her moist sex. She was more than ready for him, and he smiled as he bent to part the curls and put his lips where his fingers had been.

'Jared...' she groaned, her rapidly beating pulse only a small part of the agitation her body was feeling. 'I want you...' She took a choking breath. 'Please...'

Jared moved over her with frustrating slowness. 'Where do you want me?' he asked huskily, depositing a trail of wet kisses from her abdomen to the curve of her nape, and she fumbled to grasp his head and bring his mouth back to hers.

'I want you—inside me,' she told him unsteadily, and, reaching down, she took his throbbing fullness into her hands.

'Okay, okay...' Jared was not proof against such out-right sensuality, and, parting her legs with one hairy thigh, he eased between them. 'Take it easy,' he breathed. 'I don't want to hurt you.'

'You won't,' she assured him eagerly, and, grasping his hands, she urged him to finish what he'd started.

And, despite Jared's initial reticence, their lovemaking was as uninhibited as it had ever been. The reassurance that he loved her had freed Isobel from any restraint, and after feeling the strength of her muscles closing about him Jared was incapable of any withdrawal. He was hungry for her; they were hungry for one another; and their climax when it came was as deep and soul-shattering as either of them could have wished.

It was only afterwards when he rolled away from her that his conscience smote him. Isobel looked so pale and fragile, lying beside him; and, turning onto his side, he stroked the unfamiliar mound of her stomach with a ten-tative hand.

'You okay?' he asked huskily, and she turned her head to look at him with adoring eyes.

'Mmm,' she breathed. 'Heavenly. You?'

Jared allowed a wry smile to twist his mouth. 'Need

you ask?' He drew his lower lip between his teeth. 'I didn't hurt you?'

'Only in the most delicious way,' declared Isobel mischievously. Her hand sought his. 'I'm so glad you're here.'

'Me, too.' He was about to bring her fingers to his lips when something moved beneath his hand. 'Hey…' His lips parted. 'He moved again?'

Isobel smiled. 'Mmm. *She* does that all the time. She's just reminding us that she's still there.'

Jared gave a small smile, but his eyes had darkened. 'And you really don't mind?'

'About the baby?'

'Being pregnant,' said Jared huskily. He grimaced. 'You'll understand I have a special reason for asking.'

Elizabeth.

Isobel gazed at him adoringly, aware that he was listening very closely for her answer. Choosing her words with care, she said softly, 'As I said before, I thought it was all I was ever going to have of you.'

He cupped her cheek. 'I don't deserve you.' He groaned. 'After the way I behaved—'

'Hey.' She covered his hand with hers. 'I was the one who initiated our relationship, remember? And if we're placing blame on anyone for me getting pregnant, then I guess that's my fault as well. I let you—well, perhaps I secretly wanted this to happen all along.'

Jared's lips curved into a sensual smile. 'I could have insisted on taking precautions every time we made love,' he reminded her gently. 'But I have to admit, I'm glad I didn't now.'

'Are you?'

'You'd better believe it.' He gave a soft laugh. 'I can't deny I would have liked having you all to myself for a bit longer, but I'm not complaining.'

EPILOGUE

ISOBEL and Jared were married three months later at the Anglican church in Newcastle where Isobel had been christened twenty-seven years before.

The wedding, which was a quiet affair, with only Isobel's sister and her family, Michelle and Phil Chambers, and a couple of Jared's friends present, took place only two days before their son, Daniel George Kendall, was born. The baby had chosen to be over a week late, which meant that Isobel had had to be married in Michelle's hastily-altered wedding dress, which caused her friend to point out that there were advantages to being overweight, after all.

But it was a beautiful wedding, and although Isobel felt like a baby elephant, Jared assured her she was the most beautiful bride he'd ever seen. And, after all, his eyes were the only ones that mattered.

But the baby's imminent arrival meant that there was no time for a honeymoon, and Jared promised to take her and the baby away in the spring, when the weather was warmer. For the present, however, they were both content in just being together, and Marion had offered no objections when Jared had broached the subject of buying her half of the house in Jesmond Dene for himself and Isobel. It seemed that the lack of luck she'd had in selling it had worked to their advantage, and Isobel was looking forward to nursing her baby under the tree where she and her mother had spent so many happy hours when she was young.

To Isobel's surprise, Howard Goldman had attended the church service, too, though he hadn't trespassed on the family celebrations afterwards. Nevertheless, she knew his attendance had meant a lot to Jared, who still had a very genuine affection for the old man. Thankfully, Howard had made a good recovery from his heart attack, and although Jared admitted that there was still some bad feeling between him and his daughter, he was of the opinion that they each needed one another too much to remain permanently estranged.

The most remarkable thing was that Jared was still working at Goldman-Lewis. During his convalescence, Howard had sent for Jared and asked him not to consider leaving the company. He needed someone he knew, someone he could rely on, in a position of authority, and, although Jared had expected it to be a temporary appointment, the old man had little bitterness towards his ex-son-in-law.

In consequence, Jared had gradually taken over the day-to-day running of the firm, and had endeared himself still further by coaxing a talented young architect from a rival firm to join them. He had also ensured the acquisition of two new contracts, including one in the City of London, and, because he and Howard understood one another so well, he was able to keep the old man informed of everything that was going on.

So much so, that a couple of weeks before Christmas Howard had announced that he was going to take his doctor's advice and delay his return to work indefinitely. He didn't say he was going to retire, but the promise was there. If Jared was willing to remain at Goldman-Lewis, he was in no hurry to return.

Jared and Michelle had made their peace with one another, too, and although Isobel knew it would take some time before her friend completely trusted him, they were getting there. The baby's arrival had gone a long way to healing all wounds, and even Howard had made an excuse to come and see Isobel while she was in the hospital. The old man seemed to want to sustain a personal relationship with Jared and his new wife, and, as their parents were dead, neither Isobel nor her husband had any objections to him adopting the role of surrogate grandfather.

The final word on Isobel's relationship with Robert Dorland came from Marion, however. A few weeks after baby Daniel was born she came to see her sister and admitted that their mother had spoken to her about Isobel's adoption just a few days before she died.

'But she was not always coherent at that time,' she excused herself unhappily. 'I couldn't be entirely sure of what she was saying, and it seemed kinder to let sleeping dogs lie.'

Isobel didn't point out the fact that she could have mentioned something when she'd shown her the letters, but her relationship with Marion meant more to her than any lingering resentment over a man who clearly hadn't wanted her.

She confessed as much to Jared that evening, when she told him about her sister's visit. She had just fed the baby and, after putting him down for a sleep, she'd settled comfortably on Jared's lap.

'So you're not sorry that you never got to meet your real father?' he asked, nuzzling the soft curve of her nape with his lips. Since she'd had the baby, Jared thought his wife had become even more beautiful, and he loved her so much that sometimes he was horrified at the risks he'd taken with their relationship in the past.

'Well, I wouldn't say that exactly,' Isobel answered thoughtfully, smiling at the seductive brush of her husband's tongue. 'But it wasn't meant to be.'

'At least you and Justine got to know one another,' Jared remarked gently. 'And she doesn't resent you any more.'

'No.' Isobel nodded, remembering the card that had been delivered a week after the birth of their child. She suspected that Marion had taken it upon herself to inform their aunt of the baby's arrival, but she'd never actually admitted it. 'She seemed quite pleased.'

'I think that's an understatement,' said Jared drily, smoothing a silky curl of hair behind her ear. 'She wants you to go and see her. Will you?'

'Maybe. Maybe later, when Daniel's older.' Isobel gave him a doubtful look. 'Does that sound selfish? It wasn't meant to be. But it's hard to see how we could ever get along.'

'I think it's your decision to make,' declared Jared softly. 'We'll do whatever you want to do.'

'Thank you.' Isobel cupped his cheek. 'But, you know what? I don't think I'll ever regard her husband as my father. As far as I'm concerned, my mother and father were dead long before I started on that journey. For me, Robert Dorland never really existed. He was just someone I briefly thought I knew.'

'He didn't know what he was missing,' murmured Jared, his hand slipping into the collar of her soft shirt. He smiled as his fingers found what they were looking for and he bent to kiss her. 'Now, do you think I could have you all to myself for a little while?'

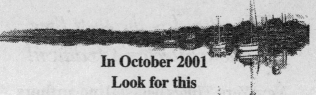

In October 2001
Look for this
New York Times bestselling author

BARBARA DELINSKY

in

Bronze Mystique

The only men in Sasha's life lived between the covers
of her bestselling romances. She wrote about passionate,
loving heroes, but no such man existed…til Doug Donohue
rescued Sasha the night her motorcycle crashed.

AND award-winning Harlequin Intrigue author

GAYLE WILSON

in

Secrets in Silence

This fantastic 2-in-1 collection will be on sale October 2001.

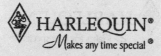

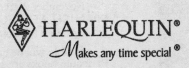

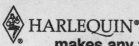